MY PART
OF HER

JAVAD DJAVAHERY

MY PART
OF HER

Translated from the French
by Emma Ramadan

Preface by Dina Nayeri

RESTLESS BOOKS
BROOKLYN, NEW YORK

Copyright © 2017 Editions Gallimard
Translation copyright © 2020 Emma Ramadan
Preface copyright © 2020 Dina Nayeri

First published as *Ma part d'elle* by Editions Gallimard, Paris, 2017

This book is supported in part by an award from the National Endowment for the Arts.

This work received the French Voices Award for excellence in publication
and translation. French Voices is a program created and funded by the
French Embassy in the United States and FACE Foundation.

French Voices Logo designed by Serge Bloch

Cet ouvrage a bénéficié du soutien des Programmes
d'aide à la publication de l'Institut français.

First Restless Books paperback edition February 2020

Paperback ISBN: 9781632062437
Library of Congress Control Number: 2019943956

Cover design by adam b. bohannon
Set in Garibaldi by Tetragon, London

Printed in Canada

1 3 5 7 9 10 8 6 4 2

Restless Books, Inc.
232 3rd Street, Suite A101
Brooklyn, NY 11215

www.restlessbooks.org
publisher@restlessbooks.org

CONTENTS

PREFACE

"Why was this country handed over to mullahs? In exchange for what? No one knows . . . Because, starting in 1979, they have been far less free, their lives more difficult than before."

In the '80s, when I was a girl, my family drove to the Caspian Sea on holiday. We rented a villa and visited the mountain villages. We gawked at Western toilets, slept under mosquito nets outside, grilled corn in the garden. We waded into the sea, the men on one side, women on the other, fully clothed. I heard my parents whispering stories of the seaside *before* . . . Women in bikinis, their black hair inking the water, couples eating smoked fish and flirting on the sand. I heard about an Iran that no longer exists, and I sensed the specter of a coming-of-age that I would never live for myself. The youthful explorations of my parents' generation, on beaches and in villa sheds and in crevices of the mountain, was a birthright yanked away over two summers in 1978 and 1979, when those same students and hot-blooded activists made an astonishing error.

It has been a jagged stone in their hearts, a collective regret, for forty years.

Like many his age, the narrator of Javad Djavahery's novel *My Part of Her* is tortured by his own complicity. At times he tries to explain it away. "The masses are desperately shortsighted and endowed with a reptilian memory," he says. "The proof is that for two hundred years, at each major turn of history, they always make the worst choices."

But his torment isn't just about an ill-fated plot to free the country from imperialism and Western plunder (goals that even the most mournful of the revolutionary generation don't disavow), but about a lifetime spent in self-preservation, betrayal, hubris, and cowardice. As a boy, he despises his kind-hearted, soft-spoken parents for their deference to the educated and the rich. At the same time, he is ashamed by their working-class trappings, the good halva and the well-washed rug. He sees himself as activist, scholar, Svengali to a circle that, over time, widens to include underground communists and revolutionaries.

Broken by his own most human instincts, he takes solace in books, and in the memory of Nilou, his mother's first cousin, after whom he lusts with the egoism and self-loathing of a child, peddling her trinkets and underthings to fellow village boys. Nilou's family escapes to the narrator's Caspian village each summer, and though he claims to love her, she is only a symbol of his class struggle and of the secrets of adulthood. She is something to possess and brandish about. He boasts when he is allowed into her bedroom, when she confides in him, when she allows him into her mind via the books he brings to her.

He is despicable and yet he has come to understand something vitally important—and he imparts his wisdom in a vitally important way.

In my work with asylum seekers I learned that their biggest hurdle is to be believed, first in asylum interviews, then in every future interaction with the Western-born. The trouble is that, to be believed, they must tell their stories differently. One asylum lawyer told me that Iranians start every story at the beginning of the universe.

And so, I chuckled when Djavahery opened like every grandfather and great-aunt and toothless uncle I've known:

"I have to start from the beginning and things often start much earlier than we think. Let me tell you a bit more about the Caspian Sea . . . "

For me, the choice is defiant, and assurance that what's coming is a true story, told in a true way, in an Iranian way. There will be no kowtowing to the Western reader in these pages. There is no room for that gaze, because this is a story about *our part in Iran's undoing*. It is a collective reckoning with ourselves, with *our* part of *her*—the monster we created.

Given that, Djavahery's artistic choices move me. His confessor's voice, situated decades later from somewhere in the West, harkens back to an old Iranian style of storytelling. The story is told to a specific person we never see, for an unstated and devastating reason we somehow understand. The unnamed narrator himself isn't a realized character so much as the universal "writer," a voice of reason, caution, experience, and shame (that very Iranian sentiment). We might even think of him as "Javad" without presuming autobiography. And then there are the archetypes: the broken boy who returns a villain; the unsullied beauty capable only of good.

A Western critic unfamiliar with our storytelling will dismiss these as unrefined—they are deliberate and, in a story shrouded in regret and altered by deep memory, powerfully true.

Djavahery is a screenwriter, and his descriptions are precise and cinematic. He describes village roads in prerevolutionary north, the young loitering "on the fenders, on the hood, sometimes even on the roof . . . It was summer, it was night, the hajji at the wheel already had a few glasses of arak in his blood. Everyone was swimming in happiness. The roads were bumpy. The cars drove slowly. The gleam of their headlights . . . illuminated in the darkness the face of your sweetheart, her silhouette, and maybe more . . . "

Though I was transported to the kind of summers that I missed, I wasn't allowed to linger, for Djavahery never fails to remind us of the catastrophe to come. "Who could have believed that the majority of those Don Juans of the summer, those youths full of promise united around a fire, writhing with laughter, telling salacious stories, quarreling for a yes or a no, showing their muscles . . . were destined for the worst suffering, for horrific deaths? That many of them would return in wooden boxes . . . That the sand would be stained with their blood, for executions would take place on the beach itself, in the calm of the morning."

And yet Djavahery hints at a horror beyond the loss of life. Something bigger has been struck down and buried. The sea, once an invitation to boundless freedom, a passage to other lands, has become a public hammam, a place of "entertainment without pleasure," without the night strolls, the bonfires, the prowling boys and joyous swimmers. The people who inhabit it are a different species. They are undead. "People who settled for the sea mutilated in this way. Summer vacationers like we had never seen before. Who were they? . . . These women who were bathing fully dressed, these men who were strolling in exclusively male groups. Not shaved, with extra-long bathing trunks."

Djavahery is unsparing in his condemnation. None of this was inevitable. This repression, the annihilation of joy, youth, and love isn't an outgrowth of misplaced idealism. It was a collective human failure, an entire country destroyed by revenge—"of the past on the future . . . The revenge of the peasants on the city-dwellers. And we, with our complicity, were only feeding the monster that was growing in the shadows, secretly multiplying."

Even so, the story ends on a seaside, in a moment brimming with hope, at the moment of one heart's triumph over a whole lot of human stupidity. It is a confession and a prayer, an ode to bygone days, a love letter to joy and sex and youth, a warning to the young, a thrilling memory of old Iran. Djavahery reminds us that men and women are destined toward ruin but also toward each other, that we must take care, as "the domain of evil is far vaster than that of good. Much more complex, much deeper."

—DINA NAYERI

MY PART
OF HER

I SAW IT ON THE WATERLINE, between the sky and the sea. You know, that fine line of foam in the morning, when it's calm, that separates the milky sky from the pale blue of the water. Oh, that blue! I don't know if you've ever seen it. I don't know if it exists anywhere else. It's a very specific blue that the Caspian reveals, on certain days, at dawn.

Barely visible, it seemed to be drifting out to sea, like an abandoned object, at an unknown distance, maybe one hundred, maybe two hundred yards away, difficult to tell in the tumult of the sea. It wasn't a lure caught in a drifting net, carried by the current, nor the back of a sturgeon come to enjoy the heat of the morning sun, nor a gray seal from Russia. No, the fishing boats didn't go that far out, and fish never remained for very long at the surface; as for seals, it wasn't the season.

I had it in my sights, and I wouldn't have let it go for anything in the world. It was morning, and I was swimming in the sea, joyful, drunk on my youth. To swim out far from the shore was a family tradition. Even a matter of local pride. We northerners love to brag about being good swimmers. The air was sweet, the weather seemed at rest. Almost completely still. As if that dawn would last forever. Not a hint of wind to disturb the silence. Just my breathing, the lapping of the water around my body, and in the distance the muffled hum of a world that I had left behind. But the sea was not calm. A sea never really is. A mysterious force continued to heave the millions of gallons of salt water up and down in a haunting motion, as regular as it was unpredictable. That force. I loved to feel it within me, near and frightening. I loved to play with it, graze it, all the while knowing that it could destroy everything if it pleased, in an instant. Everything. But not me, because I was a part of it. I was swimming, and the tranquil weather was only a facade, the hands of the universe continued to move. Suddenly, everything sped up, the solar disc broke free from the horizon, and its low rays covered the surface of the water, like thousands of stars, a wild spectacle, blinding, dazzling. During all this time, I had kept my eyes riveted to it. I didn't want to lose it. I didn't want it to disappear into the rise and fall of the swell. Between the ripples and the glistening stars. In the misleading distance of the sea. But I lost it. It disappeared, as though

devoured by the water. I swam farther out: if it was somewhere, it had to be there, but there was nothing. Only
water billowing over invisible hinges. Only the blue sky
to infinity. Only my amplified solitude. I started to swim
frantically. Chopping the waves with all my strength. I
stopped, later, out of breath. I had surely gone out too
far, I said to myself, and turned back. The sandy shore
was almost invisible. I could scarcely make out, veiled
in the morning haze, the top of the water tower. Then
the sight of land was gone, leaving nothing around me
but monotone horizons, shades of blue, as far as the
eye could see. The black stain, the small blemish on the
smooth skin of the water, had disappeared. Drowned,
erased, as though deleted from the page of the sea, as
if it had never existed. There was nothing for me to do
but turn back around like on other mornings, return to
the shore, empty-handed. But I didn't. I continued to
search the horizon. Something told me that it was there,
within reach, that it would resurface, that I had to wait.

I let myself float in the serene gravity of the water,
almost immobile, cradled by the sea, carried by the cur-
rents, waiting for time to pass, for the stars to disappear.
Gradually the sun was draped in a series of clouds. The
blue of the sea had turned darker, the light had softened,
and I found it again. It wasn't a thing that was drifting

5

with the current, but a person swimming, someone rushing in a precise direction, toward the open ocean. Quickly I resumed my crawl to catch up. And I saw her. Bingo: a woman! And not just any swimmer, but the famous morning swimmer of the Caspian herself. I let myself be carried by a gentle swell. From the top of the wave, I could better observe her. It was definitely a woman. The straps of her bathing suit were visible on her shoulders, and what had once resembled a clump of rope dragged by the current was her long black hair floating in the water, behind her neck, over her shoulders. She was swimming like a fish. Truly. She moved without displacing the water around her. Her arms, more efficient than a sturgeon's fins, cleaved the surface of the sea, softly, like a sharpened blade. I approached with great effort. When I reached her, the sun, that killjoy, blinded me. In the shimmering of the water, her image reached me sporadically, in flashes. She changed position, turned onto her back. She had seen me or had felt my presence. I yelled, in a cry muffled by the water: "Hey!" She turned toward me. She pushed her hair back so I could see her. Then I was certain. It was definitely her, Nilou. I had finally found her.

§

You're right to ask why I've come to see you after so long. You, my companion for those sad years . . . To speak to you about the Caspian at dawn, about a girl swimming in the sea? No! You're not naive. You know I'm here for another reason. You're wary. You're wondering what the point is of digging up old land, if not to awaken demons of the past. And you came here, so far from your country, for a completely different reason. To forget, right? To live another life, right? Don't worry, I'm not here to judge you. I did exactly the same thing. Like you, I wanted to turn the page, and I even believed, for some time, that I had succeeded. So much so that, sometimes, I amused myself thinking back on those years, returning to them, as one returns incognito to one's childhood village, but one day I woke up and I knew, suddenly, that things couldn't continue on as before. You'll see. It'll happen to you, if it hasn't already, and you will know as I do that the life you spent wanting to forget was in fact nothing but a life devoted to remembering. I am here because no one else can do for me what you are able to do: understand me. You will do what you wish with what I have to tell you. Apologies for revealing this truth to you so belatedly. Had I shared it with you earlier, perhaps it would have helped you to better endure the terrible burden of guilt that, I know, has always weighed on you.

I won't take long, but be patient. The truth I will confide in you is very particular. I have to start from the beginning, and things often start much earlier than we think. Let me tell you a bit more about the Caspian Sea, at dawn on a distant morning. A morning when you were perhaps not even born yet. About the sunrise. About the blue reflection of the sky over the sea. About a girl who was swimming alone, far from the coast. About the thirteen-year-old boy that I used to be. Those were carefree years. That was youth.

The swimmer that morning was my distant cousin, Niloufar, a sixteen-year-old girl, three years older than me, whom everyone called Nilou against her will. Three years apart, that's a lot at that age. You know. She was already almost a woman. And I was still a child. She was beautiful and slender. She had an elongated face and dimples on her cheeks, inherited from her mother, who was my mother's niece, even though they were nearly the same age. Niloufar had large black eyes, accentuated by a strange line, like freshly drawn kohl. Long curly hair, ebony black, and the gait of a satisfied predator. She was the most idolized girl on the coast. The most coveted, and also the most unattainable. For several summers now. Since her breasts had grown beneath her scruffy T-shirts.

Those same faded T-shirts that she stubbornly continued to wear. Since her childhood legs had lengthened in her shorts to become the long, solid, and robust legs of a young woman in full possession of her powers of seduction. Since her mere arrival in Chamkhaleh constituted the major event of the summer in the eyes of her numerous suitors. And, that morning, I had heightened the legend surrounding her by discovering that she was an even better swimmer than people said.

§

She was now within earshot. I called to her. "Hey Niloufar!" It's a magnificent name, isn't it? Niloufar, nenuphar, water lily . . . She turned around and waited for me to reach her. Surprised? Not at all.

"What are you doing here?" I asked her between two strokes. But rather than responding, she let herself sink for a few moments, then, resurfacing, threw her head back with that exquisite gesture girls use to clear the hair from their faces, and smiled at me before saying:

"I should be asking you that. I'm here every morning."

"I didn't know you went out so far." Far from the coast, I meant to say, but I stopped talking, out of fear that a slight trembling in my voice would betray my lie.

"So what?" she responded, looking me straight in the eyes.

That morning, she was even more beautiful than in my memories of the previous summer. She was floating in the blue of the ocean, as though effortlessly, her hair roaming around her shoulders like an enormous black jellyfish, and her body, slowly moving through the kaleidoscope of the sea, rendered her almost unreal. Suddenly she rolled over, plunged. Under the water, her skin shone like the scales of a strange fish. She dove, pierced through the water seamlessly, like a needle through silk. Then the hole closed up behind her. The sea returned me to my solitude. I looked around. But there was nothing. Only stretches of sea, water covering water, bathed in the sky. The sun had risen above the horizon line and the sea reflected a slightly darker blue. Since Niloufar had disappeared beneath the water, time seemed longer. I turned around, scrutinized the waves as I awaited her return, watching for her siren's hair, the gleaming skin of her shoulders, but she didn't resurface. She had simply left, without a trace. Eventually I started to worry. I dove down looking for her, I went as deep as I could, but the water was too opaque for me to see more than a few yards in front of me. Very quickly I needed air again, and I abandoned my mission, went back up. At the surface, the silence was even heavier, more harrowing. Seconds seemed to go on forever. So much so that I started to have doubts, as strange as that may seem. I must have dreamed it, or I was still dreaming. They say it happens to even the most experienced swimmers. They fall asleep in the warm water and drown in their sleep, confusing slumber and death once and for all. That thought made me panic. I wanted to wake up, but how can someone wake up when they're already awake? Then she resurfaced. In the exact spot where she had plunged, fresh, not even short of breath. She had something in her hand. She held it out to me. "Here, it's for you." It was a piece of red coral. I had never seen anything like it. She told me that she had always practiced holding her breath, and now she could hold it for more than three minutes. "Three minutes is a long time," I said to her, then we swam another hour, toward the sun, the open ocean. I kept close to her, close enough to feel her body through the rippling of the water. Close enough to hear her breathing. To feel the sprays of water cast off involuntarily by the movement of her limbs. But not sufficiently close for our bodies to touch. I reminded her that we had to head back before the sun reached its highest point, after which it would be impossible to find the coast again. Otherwise, we would have to wait another two hours. She replied that I didn't have to worry, that she knew how to get back. Without being able to explain why, she always knew where the shore was!

I believed her. After all, what bad thing could happen to me? I was near her. That was enough to render all the craziness of the world logical. We floated on our backs, let our bodies drift with the current. It was a blessed moment. The first time that I had been alone with her, that I had really spoken to her. As if the invisible wall that forever separated us had finally dissolved in the warmth of the Caspian. Later, I learned that I was wrong, that the wall, made of our differences, would not break for so little. Then the wind picked up, and the sea started to thrash around us. We had to go back. She told me to follow her and started to swim in a direction supposedly leading to the shore. I swam with her as best I could, essentially at my maximum, if I'm honest. She was doing a perfect crawl, vigorous, rhythmic, and fluid, which she maintained until the shore materialized once more on the horizon, at first as an indistinct line, then thicker, then clear. The water tower, the straw roofs, the fences between the cottages, the world of the landed. Then she slowed down her pace and we were able to speak again. I asked her when she had arrived in Chamkhaleh, insinuating that I was not up to date, that I hadn't noticed her arrival. I was lying, obviously, of course I knew when she had arrived with her family. It was, in fact, the most highly anticipated event in the village. How could I not know? She had arrived a week ago to stay, as she did every year, in Villa Rose, overlooking the sea. We had raptly followed all the stages of their moving in. The sudden liveliness of the house, the opening of the shutters, the table and chairs taken out of storage. The lights shining in all the rooms, her silhouette on the terrace, her first walks on the beach with her dog Tamba running behind her, and her solitary morning swims, which everyone spoke about without having any real proof.

For several nights, on the beach around a fire, passing around joints and drinking arak from a bottle concealed in a paper bag, that was all we spoke about. About Niloufar and her family. Those stories alone occupied the majority of our nights. Even if in my presence the commentary was draped in a light veil of modesty, more restrained, for she was my cousin after all. To be Niloufar's cousin was no small thing. It was almost a full-time job. A position that had to be maintained with a great deal of tact. Not to come across as the intolerant cousin, ready to take up arms to defend her honor, nor the indifferent cousin who lets anybody advance without rite of passage. I had become, little by little, without realizing it, the guardian of the temple, the keeper of the keys of a fortified castle that held the most coveted jewel of the coastline—Niloufar.

I have a hard time explaining the incredible attraction we felt for Niloufar at that time. Okay, she was beautiful, I've already said that. Standing tall on her legs, her black hair always loose over her shoulders, the curve of her breasts visible beneath her worn out T-shirts. The unusual appearance of a scrappy boy, but with all the attributes of a girl. There was also the mystery surrounding her family. People who shared a corner of the sea with us each year, the fine sand, the sun and the pure air of the North, all while being very different. Everyone knew it. First there was her father. A man with an odd appearance, who people referred to, in exaggerated voices, as "the Doctor." Emphasis on the second "o." He was completely bald. And yet: very young. He had been afflicted with a sort of alopecia that had made him lose all his hair. This peculiarity was the subject of jokes and stifled laughs among my aunts that as a child I didn't fully grasp. He was officially a doctor. His practice was in Rasht, the capital city of the region, sixty miles away. But his fortune didn't come from his medical practice alone. He was a businessman. A man who people whispered had connections. At the time, the expression "having connections" meant a lot of things, including, among others, to rub elbows with powerful people, which is to say having access to the Shah's inner circle. The legend was reinforced by the fact that he had served as mayor several times in that same big city, two or three terms, I can't remember. Even in my family we spoke of him with a certain fear. Always in a low voice. Involuntarily throwing a wary glance left and right. As if something about him incited worry or should remain a secret. I had heard, surreptitiously, that he had disappeared after the coup d'état during Mosaddegh's reign and lived in hiding for a few years before resurfacing to become what he was now. Even though, later on, I learned the reason behind his disappearance, his fortune, and the fear that he inspired in others, he remained, for me, an ex-fugitive, an outlaw who had turned rich and powerful. We saw him relatively infrequently. He only came to Chamkhaleh on weekends and holidays. Those were the days when bizarre vehicles surrounded Villa Rose. Big black cars often manned by drivers who, late at night, would kill time by smoking and chatting in front of the closed gate before leaving at dawn with their bosses in tow, the mysterious guests of Villa Rose. Outrageous parties, fantasized about by the locals, were in fact simply backgammon tournaments, as Niloufar's father was addicted to the game. I knew it, without ever saying so, because the rumors of debauchery were more profitable for my business. Wealth, power, an elegant mother who looked like a Hollywood starlet and who we watched on her terrace, facing the sea, drinking tea and reading, so different from the style of our own mothers. All of that made Niloufar and her family different from us. But I think what made her so desirable, so indispensable to our summers, was simply her indifference. Her indifference to the opulence in which she lived. The richer you are, the less you need to show it; and the less you show it, the more people think you're rich. She could walk around in clothes with holes in them, sneakers in tatters, or barefoot, and it didn't change a thing. She possessed the elegance of a queen. She didn't pay the slightest attention to the young men who crossed her path through a thousand ruses. Not a word, not a look, not a smile, except for that slight crease at the corners of her lips, which the others interpreted as contempt, but which I knew was only amusement. Niloufar was not a sad girl, neither reserved nor timid. Far from it. She would laugh with her friends, and most of all with her cousin Anahid, who came to spend a few weeks each summer at Villa Rose. During the summer, other female aliens arrived. Reunited, those young girls of the same age formed a joyous and boisterous band. All beautiful and, through a secret pact, all contemptuous of us boys. At each outing they sowed terror on the beach. Real outlaws.

But remember! This was Iran at the time of the Shah. You never really experienced that Iran. There was not yet even a single veiled woman on the coastline; scarves and chadors weren't worn. Instead, there were those girls, with their tiny bikinis, their tank tops, their light dresses blowing in the wind, their bursts of laughter. They wriggled their hips on the hot sand. Roared with laughter. I promise you, the bronzed women of Malibu were nothing compared to such a sight. Everything was wrecked in the wake of their cruel procession. All that was left was lava, ash, and broken hearts. And despite that, faithful to their pact, there wasn't a single breach through which the boys could have climbed, not even the most aggressive from the surrounding areas. They were all crazed, and the more desperate they were, the better it was for me. The more fervent their flame, the more successful my business, my prices went up, and I became vital. Indeed, by all accounts I was the only bridge to access the inaccessible Holy Grail of Niloufar. I was "the cousin." That's how I was introduced to someone new. "You know him? He's the cousin." Often, it wasn't even necessary to say whose cousin I was! I wore that title like a rank in the caste hierarchy. And I profited from it. Of course. Why would I have done any differently?

Discreetly at the beginning, then overtly. I profited in a thousand ways. I didn't have to do anything, it was the cruel law of supply and demand. I was the only one who was able to join the band of girls from time to time. Who had the privilege of paddling in a boat, on the water of the river, with the girls inside. Who carried the fruit basket for Niloufar's mother, handed her the apple she bit into. I had the secret password to enter the black gate of Villa Rose and to drink tea with her mother, on the terrace, in full view of everyone. Even if it was only an illusion. I paid in my own way for the privilege of being the cousin. And it was costly, much more costly than my friends could have imagined.

You know, I'm a child of the North. For me, the sea has always been the opposite of death. To die in the sea is unthinkable to me. Even today, I think that if ever, through some serious accident, I were to fall from a boat into the open ocean, I would be able to swim for as long as it took to arrive on solid ground. For me, the sea is tranquility, liberty, life. I believe that the sea could never portend anything bad for me, and on that morning, swimming toward the open ocean, while the sandy shore of the Caspian was veiled beneath the haze, I thought of everything that a young man of my age can think of, except death. Everything except suffering, abandonment, and betrayal. Because the force and the ardor of my thirteen years, the mother ocean, that calm blue, were there to shield destiny from my eyes. That terrible destiny. No, I wasn't aware of it yet. Wait a bit longer, I'll tell you, you'll know everything. But in that moment it was nothing but an ordinary morning, it was the call of youth, at the beginning of a summer full of promises. Like every morning, I had eaten my atomic breakfast. That's what we called it. Buffalo milk, sturgeon caviar, buckwheat pancakes, and fig jam. Believe me, at thirteen, with those substances in sufficient quantity in your blood, in a state nearing drunkenness, and alongside Niloufar, that strange spice, that time bomb, even the infinity of the sea and the waves far from the shore can't tire you out. In that moment, distance becomes an exhilarating adventure; risk, a playground; death, a friend. The good and the bad, game pieces in a terrible business. So guess just how far a person so falsely powerful and thus prepared to satisfy his desires can go? What price is he capable of paying? Do you have an idea?

That morning, the boy who emerged from the sea was no longer the same as the one who had entered. The one who was swimming in Niloufar's wake was someone else. I know now that my gentle Caspian was still a sea, and that morning it drowned me. The boat of my life had capsized. Another was swimming in my place, another who looked like me, but who was not me. That other had charged straight ahead. Incapable of reading this very story, although it had been written distinctly on the unfurling waves, on the sand trampled by the first passersby. Another who, with the innocence of someone drowning, the worst of the drowned, for he is unaware of his drowning, was only thinking of one thing: keeping up with that magnificent swimmer. She kept half a length ahead of me, swimming joyfully at three knots. Like a dolphin, and the distance only increased. I was thirteen years old, and I had just lost my last chance of remaining a child.

As soon as I was out of the water, I showed her my hands and my fingers, all wrinkled. She showed me hers, which were much less so. I told her it wasn't all that surprising. That of course she was more of an amphibian than I was. My flattery amused her.

"You mean that I'm a real tadpole, is that it?" she said to me, laughing, throwing her head back so that I could admire her long neck and her impeccable row of teeth. Then she invited me over to have a drink at her house, "if you have time . . . " Of course I had time. All the time she wanted. And later, in Villa Rose, I had just drained my glass of lemonade when she invited me to follow her into her bedroom.

§

She never knew that, on that morning, our meeting in the sea had been no accident, because since she had arrived, I had been watching for her every day in the stretch of sea in front of her house. A frantic quest that brought me a little closer each time, until the day when I finally found her. She couldn't have known that someone was responsible for that series of events. Me. In addition to no longer being a child, I had started to play God. A strange god just as powerful as he was weak, both omnipotent and susceptible. Without that falsely fortuitous encounter, perhaps I would never have become for her what I would later. This story would never have existed for me to recount to you. I would have remained the distant cousin from the old branch of the family tree. A cousin whose intermittent presence didn't come into contact with the life of the beautiful Nilou except for one or two times a year, without leaving much of a trace. With whom she didn't share anything more than distant memories of vacations and a few yellowing snapshots in an old album that she might have shown to her children one day, saying: "Oh, that guy, he's a cousin I saw during the summer. What was his name again?" Or something like that. I would have remained the person I was, the son of Aunt Fakhry. People liked my mother. The kind, adorable, affable Aunt Fakhry. They liked the stories she told. Stories that everyone had heard numerous times but wanted to hear again because she told them so well. Aunt Fakhry, beloved for her buckwheat halva, which people ordered in advance, to eat for Nowruz[1] and at the end of the summer. Aunt Fakhry and her curly hair, prematurely gray. Aunt Fakhry and her legendary smile and good humor. Aunt Fakhry and her house that they called "small" and "warm," in a "pleasant" neighborhood of a small "picturesque" town. "Right by the river, with a view of the mountain." All you had to do was replace "warm" with "insignificant" to get an accurate picture. But they neglected to mention that the river was dry six months of the year, that its sludge was nauseating, and that we, the locals, the happy inhabitants of this "picturesque" and "pleasant" place, never lifted our heads to look at the green side of our magnificent mountain! We had other things to do. Yes, my mother, who was loved for reasons that I hated. I hated that they could love my mother for her halva, her kindness, her good humor, and her stories. And I hated that they opened the door to

Villa Rose to me only because I was her son. We were from the other branch of the family. The ancient branch, the rotten branch. The part of the family that had remained in the little town of the North. A small town that, because of how the road maps were laid out, had found itself on the main thoroughfare that went from the capital to the seaside resorts on the edge of the Caspian. We could see the others passing through in their cars. The others who never stopped, unless they had to, who then immediately found themselves in the claws of deceitful merchants who sold them trinkets at exorbitant prices. At the time, that was considered dishonest. The concept of tourism didn't exist for us. The visitors took off again, leaving behind a few coins and the dust of a poorly distributed modernity.

The other side of the family had answered the call of the real cities. They had the audacity to leave and settle down in Tehran, then in Los Angeles, New York, and Paris, becoming engineers, senior officials, doctors, or generals in the royal army. As for us, we had stayed to guard the invisible temple of tradition, to keep the old local businesses going: grocers, jewelers, rice wholesalers, or tailors and silkworm merchants like my father. Thus my mother, according to the season and the circumstance, was the wife of a tailor whose business was between two other shops in the row of tailors, or the wife of a silkworm merchant.

That was my father's only interesting quality. Otherwise, in the row of tailors, the shops looked so much alike that I asked myself how it hadn't happened already that my father or another tailor entered the wrong door without realizing it and ran his neighbor's business. I shared my mother's confusion about his profession. I never knew whether my father was a silkworm merchant and a tailor in his off-hours, or the other way around. In any case, his valiant worms only spun their precious cocoons once a year, leaving him the time to sew during the long winters of the North, hidden away in his shop. I understood the strange link between those two very distinct professions years later, when one morning I opened his shop and set myself up in his place. That mix of two jobs made it so that he was often away from home. During the cold season, when the worms were still in their eggs, he would take the measurements for his tailor shop clients with the help of a tape measure. He would write them in a notebook, whose pages were doubled with carbon paper, and he would pin the copy on the fabric brought by the client. For the pants, he would ask the men a very important question. He would ask them whether they were lefties or righties. He wasn't talking about their hands, rather, alluding to the side to which the client typically arranged his intimate parts. He would note it down on the same piece of paper, with either an "L" or an "R" circled. My father's pants were reputed to be very comfortable. One of the rare prides of the family. Like all the tailors, he would always take on more orders for Nowruz than he was able to handle. Consequently, like all the other tailors, he was always running late as the New Year approached. He was forced to work late into the night. Those nights, I would bring him his dinner in a three-tiered lunch box, I would cross the avenue where one of every two shops still had their lights on. Behind the steamed-up windows, I would see men hunched over what would become, a few days later, a client's New Year's outfit. My father would eat quickly, in silence, too tired to speak, then he would hand the container back to me and resume his work. Often, he would sleep in his shop, on a makeshift bed, heaps of suits that were ordered and never picked up, but that he kept, just in case. In spring and summer, he was on the road, going from village to village to purchase worm farms in advance. Then he would go survey them. As soon as I was able to hold myself up on the pannier rack of his moped, he brought me along with him. He knew everything about silk and taught me patiently. It was the rare topic that made him emerge from his legendary silence. He would sit me down in the warm and muggy shade of the farms to listen to the shrieks of the silkworms. The sound of tons of mulberry tree leaves, devoured and digested by the insatiable *Bombyx mori*, then spat back out on a loop. The deafening din of the march of the caterpillars.

Yes, I would have remained the provincial cousin who knew how to be useful, carrying Nilou's mother's grocery bags on the way back from the market, paddling in the waters of the river when the whole family went to picnic on a boat, serving the halva twice a year on polished copper trays, a long frail silhouette with scrawny legs and clothes that were never the right size, stuck between his father and the edge of the frame in family photos. For Nowruz, so many people would drive their beautiful cars, the neighbors watching from their windows, squeezing into the small cul-de-sac where we lived to invade the house. Conquerors, calm, sovereign, with a quasi-colonial disdain, they would bring gifts. They were cheerful and polite. They would marvel at the garden. My mother's geraniums ("Oh, they're magnificent"), my father's orange trees ("Oh, they're beautiful"), the oranges ("Oh, they're delicious"), the watermelons and pumpkins hitched to the cracked girders of the balustrade ("Oh, they're adorable"). I was there to welcome them, dreading my father's arrival. He would come on his moped, always in a rush. It was without fail his worst period, the high season of work, either in winter, when the cuts of dark flannel, pinned with his clients' measurements, were piled on the shelves of his store, like so many promises he couldn't keep, or in summer, during the harvest of the *Bombyx mori* cocoons. These were the times when Niloufar's family wanted to eat halva at Aunt Fakhry's house, and there was nothing to do about it. When my father arrived, always late, he was a little disconcerted by his wife's family, already settled into our "charming little house," waiting to be served halva. He would greet the guests, excusing himself. For my father excused himself endlessly, for everything and for nothing. It wasn't enough for him that he did it, he forced me to do it too, to ask for forgiveness. The reason didn't matter. Then he would give me inappropriate and useless orders, to go fetch who knows what, a chair for someone who had no intention of sitting, or water for another who wasn't thirsty. His face blushed at every question they asked him, no matter how harmless, often out of pure politeness, just to make small talk. He would force himself to give the best possible response, but I knew that it was wasted breath, for they had already forgotten the question, and no one was interested in his answer. It always happened in the same way. Upon their arrival, they would set up in the courtyard, under the pretext that they preferred the garden, when really it was because they were too lazy to take off their shoes. My mother would end up inviting them in with their shoes on, a favor she only accorded two or three times a year, to important guests. They sat on the chairs arranged along the walls and ate, delighting in every bite. They were right to do so; my mother's halva was famous. Then they left, promising to return the next year. Immediately, my father, grumbling out of the corner of his mouth that his day was shot, would mount his moped in a hurry to make up for lost time at work. My mother would unwrap the presents, always the same, vases and other crystal objects, look at them with an annoyed expression for a little while, then carefully put them back in their original packaging, for the shelves and the mantel were already full of gifts from previous years. Those vases would inevitably be recycled as gifts at the next occasion, and would make a long, festive journey through the family, passing from hand to hand, ending up back at their starting point. Then my mother would take out the rugs, declared impure, sullied by the guests' shoes, lay them out in the courtyard, and wash them under running water. Soaking wet, they weighed as much as a dead donkey when I laid them out on the terrace before returning the chairs to the neighbors we had borrowed them from. The rugs dried over a few long days, the drops continuing to fall on our heads, and our "charming little

house" would go back to how it was before the Tatars
passed through. Empty, sad, uneventful.

A few days later, the photos from the visit would arrive in
the mail. A thoughtful gesture on the part of our guests.
They would be placed in the family album. One of them
was of particular importance. A family photo that my
mother demanded each time. Always in the same place
and in the same arrangement. The different vintages of
each photo, placed side by side, showed the evolution of
our lives like a strange diagram. The frame was always the
same, with the red brick wall, the row of pots overflowing
with geraniums, the sunlight at the end of the day speckled
by the orange tree branches. The only thing that changed
was the silhouettes. From photo to photo, my mother got
a bit fatter, and my father grew paler and less and less
distinct. As if the camera's focus wasn't functioning for
him. At this rate, we would have ended up not being able
to see him at all anymore.

The Doctor was also putting on weight, but remained
solidly the Doctor, with his spread legs of a Doctor, his
prominent stomach of a Doctor, his piercing gaze of a
Doctor who, even in the photo, was examining you, for
free, taking your temperature, probably through *déforma-
tion professionnelle*. Niloufar's father was someone who

knew everything. One of those people who looks at you just to remind you of that fact, and that you know nothing. The exact opposite of my father, who would always say that he knew nothing about anything and give me discreet taps in the presence of guests while raising his eyebrows, in a codified body language, to remind me that I should keep quiet like him, that I had to listen to the others like he did. Always someone else who knew more than you. Then, in the middle of the frame, Niloufar's mother, who remained unchanged. Tall and slender, shielded from time. Smiling with her large mouth adorned with her impeccable teeth. So impeccable that they were all you saw. Then at the two ends, like brackets enclosing the gathering of our parents, us. Nilou and I. We were growing eagerly, trying to escape the frame. Obliging the invisible photographer, often a cousin summoned to the rescue, to retreat a bit more each year to enlarge his field of vision. Each time unveiling a bit more of the decrepitude of the walls, the ugliness of the doors and windows, the impoverishment of our home.

I had forgotten those photos, though their trace had never been truly erased from my memory, until the day, years later, when I happened upon the old albums with the padded leatherette covers. They were arranged in a storage room behind a wobbly door, shut with the heavy padlock of oblivion. With the years, we see things differently. Through the magnifying glass of time, I was able to see those photos and all they concealed. I discovered that each of them contained two images. Two images that were completely distinct, displaced visions from two worlds, reunited in the same frame, bound by a strange invisible adhesive ribbon. In the photos, my parents and I were dressed in our best outfits, while Niloufar and her family were wearing their everyday clothes. We had the elegance of ordinary people, while they had the elegance of the rich. We were striking forced poses. They looked like themselves. Happy eaters of buckwheat halva, ephemeral guests of our humble abode. Then Nilou and I, unchanging, planted on either side of the frame, she, rather bored, me, looking haggard, and in the center, my mother and her niece, Niloufar's mother, two childhood friends, reunited once more, their shoulders brushing, the two of them staring straight at the camera. Niloufar's mother unveiling her brilliant smile, my mother her legendary warmth. And I was finally able to distinguish, nearly visible to the naked eye, beneath the glue worn down by time, the demarcation line that separated our two worlds. The two universes, so distant, whose point of connection was the two women, our mothers. Despite a thousand details that distinguished them, a secret linked them forever. Something that took me a long time to discover. Yes, the established order of history had been broken. I would not continue down the path that had been drawn for me. I would not calmly maintain my place in the family tradition. On the wrong or right side of the demarcation line.

That morning, in Villa Rose, entering Niloufar's bedroom, deaf to the alarming click of that notch turning once more in the complex mechanism of our relationship, I had just crossed a line, perhaps the final rampart, beneath the incredulous gaze of the Caspian, where in the background the first waves of an impending storm on the coast were already unfurling.

§

I was thirteen years old, and it was the first time I had found myself alone in a bedroom with a girl, and it was Niloufar's room on top of it. I can tell you I was petrified; my eyes were darting around like a fish that's been suddenly taken out of its bowl and thrown in the pool. My brain kicked into high gear. I registered everything I saw involuntarily. I observed this place with the many eyes of a strange insect. The eyes of all my peers. How many of the people I knew dreamed of being there, in my place? I breathed in the air, inhaled the perfume, and memorized the objects. The personal effects of the young girl scattered here and there. The layout of the room, the placement and geometry of the objects. I noted every detail. I registered everything. To satiate my curiosity? Not only. Because I knew that soon I would recount it all. I would give the details, this room lusted after by all my friends, so many choice goods at the end of the aisle in the front window of my shop. Then distill them in small quantities, between two puffs of hashish that they would offer me generously, or sprinkle details over the course of an anecdote, as if it had escaped from me, to watch my friends' eyes open wide, their faces withdraw, their fists tighten, and maybe even see the misplaced hand of one of them feeling his crotch. Yes, I would take everything to resell, drop by drop, at top dollar, bathed in a strange mixture of pride, amusement, and guilt.

The room was almost empty. Niloufar only stayed there a total of two months of the year. On the walls, not a single image. No photo of a singer, actor, or other manly idol, no couple intertwined in front of a sunset or any other romantic landscape common among young girls her age. No, none of that. The walls were totally bare. A few boxes piled up served as a bedside table. The bed had been pushed up against the side window. Through the other, bigger window, the sea entered the room. The bulk of the delicious disorder of her bedroom was made up of clothes, thrown all over the place. You could see the pebbles and the shells collected on the beach in abundance. A few scattered books. My eyes feverishly traversed all the corners of the room. Then suddenly stopped on a piece of lace poking out from the heap of crumpled clothes at the foot of the bed. Something that could have been lingerie. Panties? A bra? That's at least what I imagined, hoped for . . . To the right of the door, the gutted armoire revealed a glimpse of a few articles of clothing hanging from the rod. I recognized her blue dress. A long dress with straps that she would often wear during her night stroll. Over in Chamkhaleh, this night stroll was a veritable institution, a rendezvous no one would have missed for anything in the world. I have to tell you all of this so that you understand.

Chamkhaleh, our seaside resort, was constructed over the years along a strip of silvery sand, which then became its main beach. It was populated by wooden houses, bungalows with straw roofs and bamboo walls. All the houses were bordered by the river, which ran along them for a few coastal miles before eventually joining the sea. Giving the town, seen from above, the appearance of a peninsula. There were at most a hundred homes. Only a few notable ones were suitable as permanent homes. That strip of land formed a separated place with an insular ambiance, governed by its own laws. At that time, there was no bridge yet, so to access it you had to cross the river by boat. The journey cost a few cents, not much, but, over time, it added up. Cars were transported on a ferry. That crossing was a bit more expensive. The ferries didn't run at night. From late afternoon until sunrise, we felt as though we were cut off from the rest of the world. A feeling that was reinforced by the insular ambiance of the peninsula. Later on, they built the bridge, and then the cars and the tourists from the capital started arriving en masse. The longtime residents still talk about that time. They recall with regret and nostalgia the era of the ferries, the boats, and the simplicity of Chamkhaleh. No electricity and no running water. Chamkhaleh was only lively for two months of the year, but what months they were! It was like those two months didn't belong to the same calendar as the other ten. Even the most traditional families loosened the reins on their children. The storekeepers and the most respected bigwigs walked around in their shortened pajamas in the garden, showing off their hairy chests and legs. Their wives wore colorful clothes, their scarves slid back a bit on their heads. Slightly more skin was exposed to the sun and to the gaze of others. We listened to music and laughter. The bottles of arak circulated in secret—even in the homes of those who went to the prayer each Friday. It was the time for summer love. It was like a sort of carnival that lasted sixty days, at the end of which we took off our masks, put our clothes back on, became teachers, shopkeepers, weavers again, or, like my father, tailor-merchants, until the next summer. At night, after the sunset, this summer population went out like an army of shadows to invade the seashore.

Our future Mecca, "Vaveli," didn't exist yet. It appeared a few years later. The history of Vaveli is important, I'll tell you about that, too. Because the village didn't have electricity, at night we were guided by torches or small gas lamps. Thus, that strip of land, barely a few miles long, cloistered by the mouth of the river and protected by the warm summer nights, was where the most joyous lovers' games of our lives took place. During these nocturnal exoduses, everything happened by feel. The lovers had to find each other, had to know how to recognize the object of their desire blindly. It was an art. You had to speak the language of the night, send signals with your torch, sing, position yourself well, have a strategy, guess at movements, calculate trajectories to find yourself in the right place at the right time, then exchange a look or a smile at the opportune moment, pass a love letter or, for the bold, steal a kiss—and amidst all that, Niloufar's blue dress, so recognizable, was of the utmost importance. She only wore it at night. Why, we never knew. A long dress, with a low, sweeping neckline. We searched for it at night, on the dirt paths. On the humid sand at the edge of the sea. The blue of her dress shone beneath the headlights of the few cars that circulated on the shoreline. The wealthy big-wigs bringing their families out. At that time, there were a lot of American cars on the road, Chevrolets, Cadillacs, with long solid hoods the girls could sit on without fear. Young people were all over. On the fenders, on the hood, sometimes even on the roof. The adults were in the cars themselves, father at the wheel, mother in the passenger seat, sometimes wrapped in a chador, but a chador that was purely for posterity's sake, with cheery colors and patterns, often sliding down onto her shoulders. It was summer, it was night, the hajji[2] at the wheel already had a few glasses of arak in his blood. Everyone was swimming in happiness. The roads were bumpy. The cars drove slowly. The gleam of their headlights was the source of fleeting bliss; it illuminated in the darkness the face of your sweetheart, her silhouette, and maybe more, depending on the intensity of the backlighting and the thickness of her summer dress. Countless palpitating, ephemeral apparitions. Once Niloufar and her friends arrived, things took another turn. The Doctor's car became the vessel of all desire, the point of confluence of all lust, a moving diamond recognized by its shine, the sound of its motor, and, especially, its blue flag. In Chamkhaleh, that second, nocturnal life was even more important for us than the first. If daytime brought the joy of swimming and showing off our skin, the sun and games, night was the realm of dreams, the infinite kingdom of the imagination, of love and desire. The lost moor where everything was possible. It lasted as long as it lasted. We squandered our sleep without keeping track. We weren't stingy with our youth. Then it all faded on the sixtieth day of summer vacation. As if the tear-off calendar of this country only lasted sixty pages. The last page was torn off with the first rain of autumn. The festivities ended suddenly, taking everyone by surprise. The exodus began in the opposite direction. We woke up with a hangover. We dropped everything, unconsummated love affairs, unfinished stories, like so many gaping wounds. We put everything in the deep freeze to be brought out again the following summer. Everything was repacked in no time. The pickup trucks were back in business. The village emptied as if it had been suddenly infected with the plague. But the love affairs remained fresh, the wounds kept bleeding, and the tears stayed warm. They were merely put in a state of suspension for the ten months that would now have to pass, as quickly as possible, until the next summer. Back in town, like our parents who were changing their clothes, we, the young, were disguising ourselves once more as high schoolers, as children of good families, no one brought up our nightly escapades. Struck by a strange amnesia, we behaved once more like strangers. As if the stories of the summer had been written in chalk, washed away, effaced by the autumn rain. The love letters, the stolen kisses had never existed. As if, during the nights of love, that carefree land had been populated by other people. It was a tacit pact, respected scrupulously by us all.

§

I'll remind you that I was barely thirteen years old, and she, sixteen. It was an important age difference, as demonstrated by the family photographs from the years in question. Niloufar was easily a head taller than me. She had all the attributes of a woman, while I was still a little boy. I had the thin body of an adolescent, the frail shoulders and the still-smooth, sad legs of a skinny kid. I didn't shave yet. The peach fuzz discolored by the sun on my chin didn't impress anyone, and the fact that I knew how to get hard and even masturbate was still an untellable secret. In sum, I was a kid; she was a woman. And once in her bedroom, I felt this reality and all its cruelty. Niloufar handed me a towel, changed in a neighboring room, and jumped on the bed, dressed in one of her typical worn T-shirts and cut-off jeans. At ease, lying on her back, legs spread, as relaxed as a woman could be in the presence of a child, or a eunuch, someone who is not in the running. No, I was not in the race. Her spread legs, the deep valley between her breasts, her belly button that her ridden-up T-shirt exposed without her paying any attention, all served to remind me of that reality. I don't know how long I remained there, stupefied, speechless, trying somehow to cling to something. But there was nothing. The emptiness had filled me. The more time passed, the less I existed. I realized that I was taking up less and less space in the room and, at that rate, if I didn't do something about it, I would soon disappear. Just like my father who would become transparent, then invisible, at our gatherings. I was about to burst into tears. I was able, I remember, with great effort, to gather my spirits. I had to do something, anything. I started to move. Transgress the invisible circle drawn around my feet. The punishment corner for the sins committed, not by me, but for which I was paying the consequences. The congenital honesty and the pathological abnegation of my father and the unlimited kindness and warmth of my mother. The harmful virtues of my parents. The phobias and the softness of my lineage. I was a young sprout on a dead branch. Roots buried in black, infertile earth. The circle that enclosed me was perfect, without a break, opaque. A line, only visible to my eyes, like a high and thick wall erected just for me. Yes, once more, I had crossed the line. I had even dared to touch things from the other world, open a few books, move a few objects. On the windowsill, the same window from which I would look out at the sea years later, through broken glass. There she had displayed some of her underwater treasure: shells, pieces of coral and pebbles of all colors, covered with dried algae. "I didn't know that the Caspian had red coral," I said. She told me that in order to see it, you had to go even further than where we had been, and you had to know how to dive. She said it without bragging, in a way that was purely informational. Then she grabbed a big book with lots of drawings and began to flip through it with the boredom of a young woman in her bedroom. After a while, the expression had vanished from her face. She seemed completely absorbed by her book. She was no longer paying attention to me. By ignoring me, she had started to turn back into what she had always been: a distant cousin, in all senses of the term. I had finished my lemonade, I had dried off, I could thus go back to my world. Which is what I did. Except, just before I left her room, she called me back, sitting up on her bed, the book still open in her hands, staring at me with a strange look.

"Can I ask you something?" she said to me.

Obviously! She could ask me anything she wanted. Anything at all. The magic had worked, she was interested in me, even asking me something. She who never asked me anything. She who was so thoroughly self-sufficient, to the point of seeming indifferent to the matters of this world. Standing motionless at her bedroom door, I was all ears, as you can imagine.

Of course, after that, we swam together again, Nilou and I. I often found myself with her, in the sea or elsewhere, in other situations, sometimes even for entire nights, in that bedroom, then in her bedroom in town, but nothing ever equaled those first moments. You see, after so many years, those are the moments that still come to mind. That encounter, a fake coincidence in the sea, that long morning of swimming, then that image, her on the bed, hair still wet, her faded T-shirt with the hole in the left shoulder, the joyous disorder of the room, the gleam of the blue dress in the shadow of the armoire and the book she was flipping through, absorbed, absent. Yes, I go back to that image often. You know why? Because until that morning, until the precise moment when I stood at the threshold of her bedroom, one foot in and one foot out, waiting for her to finish her thought, for her to ask what she wanted to ask, I still thought that everything was possible. I had hope. I thought that the world could still belong to me. I even had a very specific plan. I knew my strengths. I had a very good memory, I was intelligent enough, and I also had a gift. A strange power, and I was just waiting for one thing: the opportunity to use it.

Among all of Niloufar's suitors, two stood out from the rest. They emerged from the pack for diametrically opposed reasons, but reasons that were just as valid. The two of them had put so much distance between themselves and the rest, that the other admirers considered themselves "disqualified." They had all put their own hopes on the back burner and made a truce, in the way one respects the primary results in a political party. Since then, all eyes were fixed on the strange duel that was taking place between the two remaining suitors. I have to go into a bit more detail for you to understand just how different they were.

The first was named Parand. He was a good-looking guy, from a good family, rich—he ticked all the boxes.

Well raised. Reddish, long curly hair, rather tall, at least six foot, and always dressed well. He had a motorcycle; he was the only one who did. But at night, he sometimes came home at the wheel of his father's Mercedes, which he drove without a license, and let us climb on the hood for a drive. We would taunt the girls. He was athletic and muscular, with the flat stomach of a teenager, and, to top it all off, he was very good at volleyball. The volleyball net was set up in a strategic location, perfectly visible from Villa Rose. Nearly every night, before sunset, the match would be in full swing. The boys would go at it hard, even more so when the girls were on the terrace. Parand always played with his shirt off. They let him have his preferred position facing the house. He was confident, bursting with testosterone and the illusions of youth. He struck the ball with force, and, when he made a point, he would throw a furtive glance at Villa Rose, as if a point noticed by Niloufar was worth double. His pockets were full of daddy's money, which he spent generously on his friends, and especially on me. It goes without saying that, by all accounts, he was very well positioned to seal the deal, to settle the score with my cousin. That's how they talked when I wasn't around. As if the Niloufar "affair" had become a collective conquest through Parand. Parand represented the local alpha male who had to defend the virile honor of our town, put at risk by the haughty indifference of the foreign girl. It was the moment when, in the collective unconscious, darling Nilou, the beloved, became the floozy who had to be dragged to bed, at whatever price. No, really, something had to be done, the affront had gone on for too long, it was urgent and Parand was the flag bearer, the valiant knight, the hero chosen for the task.

The other suitor was also from a well-off family, but his was more traditional. He wasn't ugly, and he dressed rather well. But he had distinguished himself and had earned the coveted place of official suitor for an entirely different reason: his unconditional love for Niloufar. He was the perfect candidate. A true romantic icon. As though ablaze with the literature of our country. Tragic, transfixed, naive, and desperately masochist. An unrequited Romeo, Majnun without Layla, who spent his days and nights outside Villa Rose, tirelessly, and followed Niloufar like a dog. He had earned a nickname. They called him *Sag-e Sani*, do you get it? "The second dog," literally. He had accepted this nickname without offense, like all the other humiliations that were inflicted on him because of his limitless love. He never said a word. Never showed any sign of weariness. He dug himself deeper every day into that tragic spiral. The more he was singled out, the more he became the laughingstock of everyone, the happier he seemed. As if it would end up bringing him closer to his goal. He accepted his circumstances as expiation, asceticism. Even if, through a tacit and collective belief, he was the person least suited to aspire to Niloufar's love and the accomplishment of the "task," his stubbornness, his constancy, and his sacrifices had in the end commanded respect and placed him in the second position in the rank of official suitors. The podium had only two levels. At least, that's what everyone thought. But that poor boy's misfortunes didn't end there, for he had two other major handicaps. First, his name was Mohamad-Réza. Compared to "Parand," this name was an enormous burden. Also, he stuttered. Not just a little. He really stuttered, tripping terribly over certain words. And by a stroke of bad luck, he stumbled over Niloufar's first name every single time. When he tried to pronounce it, it was like he was hurtling down ten flights of stairs headfirst, with his "Ni-ni-ni-ni-ni" becoming more and more painful, more and more jolting. As if he were smashing his skull on each of those stairs, letting loose an unending "ni." As if he were losing his breath, like a tire pierced to the rhythm of the "ni"s that escaped his mouth, to the point of collapse, to the point of death. That was when the most cynical of the boys swallowed their derisive smiles and kept quiet, for we were all hanging from his lips and hoping for only one thing: for him to finally spit out that damn name and move on to something else. Mohamad-Réza had an advantage, though, negligible in the eyes of others, but important nevertheless. He had a beautiful voice and sang very well. Paradoxical, isn't it? The same part of his body was both his advantage and his downfall. For, as is often the case with stammerers, he never stammered while singing. When he sang, he was beautiful. We realized that what he sang wasn't chosen at random, but always related to a certain subject. He who was often silent expressed himself through song and thus made up for his moments of stolen speech. This was how he participated in debates, shared his vision, gave his opinion; he existed through the language of song. He knew by heart a river of couplets, a Caspian of poems, through which he could express practically anything. One night, I remember, faced with the mockery of his friends because of a word he had struggled over, he cut off his sentence and suddenly broke into song. It was really something. He threw back his head, unleashed his magnificent voice, his two fists squeezed tight along his body like a soldier, and literally wailed a poem by Hafez. His voice was so powerful, so lofty, that it gave us all goosebumps. I remember that we remained silent for a long time after he had finished singing and got up to leave, tears in our eyes.

In my role as a go-between, a modem, hub, and transformer linking Niloufar to the world of the boys, I inevitably dealt with Mohamad-Réza, too. My schedule included hours of walking with him, at night on the warm sand, along the river, in the winding alleys of the village, never far from Villa Rose. Listening to sad songs that he hummed and, on the seashore, on the hills of sand, I would watch strange birds fly from his throat and always take off toward his reason for being, his Mecca, his Nilou. I let him cry on my shoulders. I have to admit, I accepted his generosity toward me, sometimes even simply out of fairness. Like an arbiter bound to remain impartial. When I could, I would give him her day's schedule so that he wouldn't have to wait uselessly in front of Villa Rose when she wasn't there. So that he could be in the right place at the right time a bit more often to see her pass. He would reward me with a pack of American cigarettes, a bottle of whiskey stolen from his father's stash, or a simple thank you, broken and tearful.

Around the fire, the night after the swim, I had a lot of things to tell my friends. Already, before I had even left the villa, I had established a palpitating sequence in my head. A few juicy details about the meeting, which I would reveal, without saying too much, to avoid provoking a traffic jam at the sea in the morning, then two or three things about the bedroom, leaving many details in the dark. Details that my false modesty didn't permit me to reveal. The imprecisions were obviously voluntary. To prolong the suspense, fan the flame of desire. Then, over glasses of arak and puffs of hashish, I would pretend to let myself go, manifest more signs of opening up all while letting the others reenter the fray and make the advances, more and more insistently. I would give in. End up describing Nilou's bedroom and the objects in it. The tape player, the music it played, the name of the singer, the CDs, the books on the shelf, the photos of her friends on the walls. Yes, that night and the nights to come, that's what I recounted, but, obviously, it was all fake. Not a word about the blue dress, the view of the sea from the window, her lying on the bed, the shifting line between her breasts, I said nothing about any of that. Not out of modesty, nor out of frugality, but simply because those details belonged to me alone. Toward the end, pretending to be evasive by changing the subject, I let slip the plan to picnic and gather fresh blackberries. Uttering those words, I suddenly became the most powerful being on the coastline, the true kingmaker, for they had all been awaiting this news. Everyone knew that once or twice during the summer, when they were reunited, all the girls spent a day picnicking on the riverbank and that the place the blackberries grew was only accessible by boat. They also knew that, to take Niloufar, her mother, and her friends, you needed more than one boat and so, in addition to me, another rower was needed. And naturally it was up to me to designate that lucky person from among my friends. Everything unfurled exactly as planned. While I was talking, I saw a strange gleam in Parand's eyes, while Mohamad-Réza kept his head down, staring at the fire that was slowly going out, stone-faced and sullen. He did nothing but listen. He nursed no hope. He asked for nothing.

At night, when I masturbated, I tried not to think about that bit of black lace I had seen in Nilou's bedroom, another detail I had jealously kept secret, but, of course, the more I forced myself not to think about it, the more I thought about it. It spun in my head and obsessed me. I wound up ejaculating into the stitches of that strange fabric, whose image was closing in on me little by little like a net.

She had signaled to me just before I left. Sat up on her bed, staring at me with her big black eyes that looked like they were enhanced with a natural mascara. Me, standing at her door, ready to leave, determined to go back to my world on the other side of the walls of the villa, to ask me what? A name. Why him? I didn't know the answer yet. Women's hearts were a mystery to me, and Nilou's heart an even bigger mystery.

Okay, I was only thirteen years old. I was just a kid. I can understand that, but did that diminish the weight of my actions? My betrayals? For I betrayed. There's no other word for it. As young as I was, I knew how to count, to measure, to anticipate. I knew how to recognize my interests. And it was in my interest not to reveal the truth that Niloufar had confided in me that day, in her bedroom. I had the choice, and I chose. I had decided to do what I had to do to allay my conscience. I didn't hesitate. My decision was categorical and flawless. No, once more, the person who emerged from Villa Rose that day was not the one who had entered a few hours before. He was walking on the shards of his childhood, too quickly shattered. On the ashes of his hopes, suddenly burned. Someone who looked exactly like me. But who was no longer me. Or rather, I had become him.

A few days later, we went to collect wild blackberries. I asked Parand to accompany me to steer the second boat.

We split the passengers, and the belle found herself in his boat. The girls were happy. They sang and had fun. Niloufar was wearing a white tank top and a pair of her old jeans cut off just under her butt. Her legs, two golden arcs, hung over the hull of the boat. Blaming the heat, Parand rowed bare-chested, thus showing off his large shoulders, his luxurious chest hair, and his bulging muscles. Stationed at the back of the boat, he rowed with regularity and dexterity. He was handsome, nice, well-mannered, smiling, and foolish. Submerged up to his neck in the pit of his useless efforts. Niloufar remained impassive before his attributes and her friends followed suit. No one paid the slightest bit of attention to the undeniable charms of my friend Parand. Niloufar even seemed a bit put off by that display of virility. I saw it in her long moments of silence, when she would stare at something invisible on the surface of the water, or in the distance, on the sandy edges of the banks. Only Niloufar's mother, who was part of the expedition, seemed interested in him. Out of politeness or perhaps out of pity. She offered him something to drink, let him carry her basket, asked him questions about himself and his family, and on the way back thanked him for his help.

The baskets were filled with excellent, juicy blackberries. The girls were having a great time, they took off with laughter and chatter. Parand was also delighted.

On the way back, he even let me drive his motorcycle. He believed that he had taken a decisive step that day. One or two more opportunities and he would be victorious, he said. I was in wholehearted agreement, interpreting Niloufar's silence as interest and timidity. Parand was over the moon. Intimidating Nilou was no easy task. He would recount it all around the fire, passing a large lump of hashish, stuffing everyone with grilled corn and sour cherry juice, celebrating his victory with his friends. I had to remain distant. Agree only as much as was necessary. Backing Parand's claims, but tacitly, so as not to appear as a mere matchmaker.

Opposite me, on the other side of the fire, Mohamad-Réza had his head lowered like he usually did. He was listening to the boasting of his rival with his legendary abnegation. As if the trophy brandished by his adversary was magnified even more in the abyss where he liked to lose himself. He was a hopeless lover, feeding off of his own tragedy. A sailor that wasn't looking for safe harbor, but for his beautiful ship. He eventually raised his head so I could see the flames burning in the watery reflection of his eyes. He unleashed real tears later that night over my shirt, in large, drunken sobs.

§

Remember what you said to me one day, in that prison. You said these exact words, about one of your numerous trips to the interrogation room: "That day, my soul lost its way." Do you remember? You told me how they had broken you into a thousand pieces. I could imagine the rest. I knew what they could do to get things out of you. What they were capable of. Putting a man in such a state. It must not have been a pretty sight. They had tortured you, that's certain, but they had also broken you on the inside. It wasn't just physical, but moral. They had reached you in your being, hurt the deepest part of you. To such a degree that you said your soul had gone astray. It was clear. All I had to do was look in your eyes when you talked about it, head lowered, empty stare. But you said it. That night, you told me everything. You told me how you had sat yourself at the table to confess everything to them. Not knowing that over the course of your terrible story you would become a bit more honest, more human, with each phrase, and I, more dishonest and less human. You told me that you had blurted out everything you remembered. About yourself and about all those around you. From how you had looked up your teacher's skirt when you were eight years old, to the names and addresses of your friends. You told them everything. You had thrown yourself into my arms to seek consolation and forgiveness.

I forgave you, even if it wasn't mine to give. But I gave it to you, the attentiveness that one human can give to another human. You told me that after that, you curled into a ball and slept for several days. Like a baby. Some indulgent friends had fed you, given you water, and you had slept. A comatose sleep. I knew that state. I had experienced it too. I knew that at that moment you were seeking death. I had sought it, too. That heavy, endless sleep was, for you, the foretaste of death. Then, one day, you got up. You accepted and assumed your new status in prison. Your role as traitor. Snitch. You wore it with dignity, with elegance even. Yes, I can say it. You continued to wear it with a great deal of elegance. You suffered. I know. It was visible in your eyes, in the lines of your face, in your hunched back. Then that suffering faded. Not suddenly, but gradually, over time. Or else it was there, but had lost its intensity. By confessing your betrayal, you were necessarily less of a traitor. While I, during all that time, was doing the opposite. I was hiding my betrayal, and because of it, I was doubly treacherous. I had no shoulder to cry on. No way to expiate my pain in the disgust of my fellow prisoners. Purify myself by rinsing off in the spit of the righteous. I was pretending. With you, with my friends, my cellmates, even my torturers. Day and night. Even in my nightmares. Those poor torturers didn't even know anymore why they were torturing me. To make me betray someone or because I had betrayed someone? In any event, by turning me into a martyr, a hero, they were only muting my true betrayal. Your soul found its orbit. Little by little, by sheer force of will, a thirst for life, and the courage to face your own truth, your fellow prisoners eventually accepted you. But not mine. My soul was without an orbit. That lasted years. All those years that separate us from the Gohardasht Prison.[3] Today, I came to you so that you would help me, so that you would listen to me. Accept this truth that I owe you, and perhaps so that you will be able to offer me your shoulder in exchange so that I might finally cry in my turn. So that my soul, too, will perhaps be able to find its way again.

Mohamad-Réza was a young, sturdy man. He was someone who possessed an innate physical force. I had never seen him exercise. He didn't play volleyball, soccer, or the other sports boys liked, but he was naturally strong. Everyone knew. For example, he was able to grab someone who was mocking him a little too much, and hold him at arm's length for several long minutes, or fight several people at once when a squabble broke out. So we paid attention to him. But our strengths always contain a weakness. His physical force and his natural resistance would later play tricks on him. Later, delirious, that strength pushed him much further than someone with a normal constitution. That night, after the fire was put out, I steered him toward his aunt's summer cottage, where he was staying during vacation. I hadn't noticed that, as he listened to the detailed story of the picnic and his rival's antics, he had guzzled an entire bottle of arak on his own and was completely hammered. On the way back, he stopped twice to throw up, but nothing came out. I had rarely seen him that wasted. The night air was still warm, he was sweating in big beads and couldn't breathe. I asked him to sit down and wait for the effect of the alcohol to dissipate, but he wouldn't listen to me. He kept walking and swaying dangerously. It was a dark night, with no moon, and I was having a hard time orienting myself. At that time, the village had not yet done away with its anarchic construction. Each person demarcated their parcel of land with barbed wire fastened to wooden posts, dug a well, planted a few trees, then constructed a shed, the minimum required to claim and validate the ownership of the land. For that reason, the roads leading to the lands didn't obey any law, forming a labyrinth to get from one point to another. I was leading Mohamad-Réza haphazardly through those dark mazes. He was stumbling and grabbing constantly onto the posts of the barbed wire. I had just located his aunt's house when he stopped and suddenly started to hurl. Then, taken over by a sort of convulsion, he turned around and started walking in the opposite direction. I grabbed his hand and hung onto his shoulders, trying to stop him, but nothing worked. I couldn't even slow him down. He wasn't fighting against me, he was simply advancing, ignoring my efforts, carrying the weight of my body without changing his speed, unwavering, like a tank. I immediately understood: he was walking toward Villa Rose. I feared the worst. Not able to stop him, I started to walk with him, trying to reason with him. Promising him everything and anything. It was useless, he wasn't listening to me. After a few minutes, Villa Rose appeared facing the sea. It had been constructed on a plot without any house opposite, leading directly onto the beach. It was not surrounded by barbed wire, but was one of those rare houses to be protected by a brick wall. It was to our left, but the erratic geometry of the roads required us to make several detours to get there. Mohamad-Réza's shouts had turned into twitchy moans. Like the wheezing of an asthmatic having an attack. Seeing the villa, he markedly increased his pace and started walking straight toward it, freeing himself of the detours that the posts and barbed wire enclosures imposed on us. He was moving in a straight line, like a cannonball. He tore off the barbed wire and the posts that were in his way, without paying any attention to the needles that stuck to his clothes, tearing his shirt and pants. Behind him, I remained a powerless witness to his madness. He was finally stopped by the clump of tangled wire around his feet. After having torn and dragged an impressive amount, he fell down. Exhausted. He was barely a few dozen yards from the villa. Behind the brick wall, a window was illuminated. A shadow was moving in a dimly lit room. Mohamad-Réza was on the ground. He was moaning with less rage and more pain. His shin was bleeding, captured in the vise of the barbed wire. I realized that this shirt was also stained with blood. On the ground, his head was turned toward the window. His neck was stretched half upright. A few minutes later, in the house, the light went off, the shadow disappeared, and the young man let himself fall down, emptied, inert.

Mohamad-Réza had other moments of crisis. Sometimes violent, but he'd never really lost his head before. I spent a long hour liberating his leg from the jumble of barbed wire. Then he followed me in silence, stumbling imperceptibly because of his wounded shin. At the entryway of his aunt's cottage, he turned toward me, placed his head on my shoulder, and unleashed a deluge of tears punctuated with silent sobs. The next day, he returned to the beach, calm as always, shaved and well dressed. He took his place again on the embankment opposite the villa, eyes riveted to the black front gate, keeping watch for Nilou's exit to follow her during her first walk of the day, keeping the required distance from her, in the wake of Tamba the dog . . .

We burned our youth to the rhythm of the passing days. Our sun rose each morning, relentless. The tongue of waves licked the beach and stirred the sand as it had always done. Our days were sweet and brimming with our indolence, our youthful experiences, our happiness within easy reach. We smoked excellent Afghan hashish, we drank alcohol that went down easy, and the boldest among us stole brief embraces in the summer nights. Everything seemed unchangeable, promised for all eternity. Time was given to us like all of life's other delights. Like the sea, like the river that flowed tranquilly and protected us from the intransigence of old laws. But something had already started to change. Muffled rumbles were rising from the depths of history. Something was afoot, unbeknownst to us. Like a volcano in the making, silently growing in the marine depths. A leviathan lurking in the obscure cavities of our country. Time was running out, and we had not yet noticed. We were positioned on a tectonic fracture, an immense fault line that would soon burst open. Even if a wise man had predicted it, no one would have believed it. Who would have imagined that our time was up? That there would be no more summer? That they would take the sea from us to wall it, to divide it in two? What spirit, what force was capable of undertaking such a project? Who could have believed that the majority of those Don Juans of the summer, those youths full of promise united around a fire, writhing with laughter, telling salacious stories, quarreling for a yes or a no, showing their muscles, burning their testosterone, then making peace to quarrel again, were destined for the worst suffering, for horrific deaths? That many of them would return in wooden boxes from a war as deadly as it was absurd, to be buried amidst the tears and moans of their loved ones? That the sand would be stained with their blood, for executions would take place on the beach itself, in the calm of the morning. They would stand one against the other with daggers drawn, not in jest, but to kill each other. Ahmad would shoot Bijan, his best friend, at point-blank range. And yet they had been drinking from the same bottle, passing the *calumet* of hashish, laughing uproariously, mouths wide open, twisting in every direction. Ahmad would close his eyes at the fateful moment, just before pulling the trigger. Bijan wouldn't be able to do anything, his eyes blindfolded and his hands tied behind his back. No, really, who could have imagined?

§

Sometimes, at night, I still return to that fire. I watch the smoke climb toward the stars. I listen to the Caspian unfurl on the sandy shore. I look at the face of my comrades in the dancing light of the flames. I know now that that campfire was the inferno of *The Raft of the Medusa*, and I'm the only survivor. Yes, me. I was the most qualified to survive, for I knew how to feed on the flesh of others.

That year, Anahid the half-German cousin arrived earlier than usual. She lived between Tehran and Düsseldorf. Each summer, she showed up in Chamkhaleh like a new arrival, and the years changed nothing. Like an alien fallen from another galaxy. She rediscovered everything. The sea, the sand, the house, the boys. Each time, I had to introduce myself as if we were meeting for the first time, or as if I too were just arriving, from a faraway place. Eventually, to help her remember who I was, I would allude to my mother. She remembered Aunt Fakhry.

"Oh, Aunt Fakhry! And her, and her . . . " " . . . Halva," I came to her aid, murmuring under my breath, "her fucking halva." "Yes, halva," she exclaimed. She adored my mother for the same reasons as everyone else. Then she left at the end of vacation and, the next year, she didn't remember any of it, and we had to start all over again. Even the fact that her father and I had the same name didn't make a difference. Once I suggested that she use it as a mnemonic device, she laughed and agreed, then promptly forgot. She was very beautiful. Her Iranian father's olive skin and her German mother's blonde hair were a good combination. Around her, we changed register. Everything was cranked up a notch. And, sometimes, several notches! First of all, she wore the tiniest bikini on the south coast of the Caspian. She was also incredibly noisy. You could hear her from morning to night. Thanks to her, everyone knew the hours of Villa Rose. Alarm, breakfast, dinner, curfew, and so on. She hovered around the boys. Not to flirt, or to escape, no, she was drawn to the boys naturally, because where she came from, there was no demarcation line between the sexes as there was for us. But how to explain that to my poor friends? While Niloufar had only two suitors, my German cousin had a hundred. She would ask one of those young bipeds to do her a favor, give her an address, a balloon, a log, then she would thank them, with a smile or a wink, and they would interpret it as an advance and immediately feel invested with the mission of Anahid's devoted servant. It was completely out of control. In a surge of maternity, Niloufar's mother had asked me to take care of her: "Make sure they don't bother her too much. She doesn't know the etiquette here." I had noticed . . . "The etiquette here," she had said, not "our etiquette"! An impossible mission. Anahid wanted to play volleyball and asked me to include her in one of the teams. I couldn't do anything but comply, otherwise I would have been lynched. On top of it she played marvelously well, jumped high, and hit hard. Her strikes were unstoppable. Due as much to the precision and the power of her hits as to the distraction her feminine charms exerted on the opposing team's defense. Each of her trips brought with it a few weeks of general euphoria. During the day, she made the boys happy. A delight for the eyes all riveted on her round bottom, when her bathing suit slid below the tan line, where the brown of the sun ceded to the natural pink of her flesh. And at night, she brought joy to the erect penises, which unleashed an abundant torrent of sperm in her honor. Sperm, the lifeblood of our youth.

That year, like the years before, her arrival had kicked everything off, and the villa had gradually filled with its other beautiful guests. Once more, the band of girls had operated as an army of invaders. A procession that trampled the coastal land and sowed a joyous discord, whose movements were followed by the opposite side with great interest. The summer unfolded at its usual rhythm. Parand, as always, played volleyball with his chest exposed, offering his most handsome appearance in the presence of the girls. I continued for my part to go about my business. Things were going very well for me. With Anahid and my new mission as her protector, I had added one more string to my bow. The boys were nearly fighting to be near me, to buy me things, to make me happy, in the hope that I would facilitate the task for them. I took advantage of their generosity without making any promises, without the obligation of any result. Mohamad-Réza remained outside of this fuss. Imperturbable, he never paid the slightest bit of attention to other girls, not even a glance at the swaying butts or the swinging breasts. For him, there was only Nilou. He was satisfied with the view at the top of the embankment. During the day, it was his designated spot, we ceded it to him without any argument. He had won it through faithfulness and punctuality, like a beggar at his place at the entrance of the bazaar, paying his tribute by accepting insults and laughs. No one dreamed of taking it away from him. It was quite simply unthinkable. At night, he had another lookout spot, but no one knew about that one. He had succeeded in keeping it a secret from everyone, except for me. Naturally. I was the one who had revealed it to him.

Even today, I ask myself why I did that. For a few puffs of hash, which I wasn't even addicted to? For a skewer of lamb? To take a ride on his motorcycle or to drive Parand's father's car? Certainly not. Was it for the money that Mohamad-Réza lent me without ever asking me for it back? No, I don't think so. We weren't starving in my house. My pocket money was enough for the needs of a thirteen-year-old boy. The real reason for my actions was something else, something deeper, more intoxicating. It was the search for power. Hardly out of childhood, I had found myself in possession of an incredible skill. A magical power. People who in normal circumstances had no regard for the child I used to be were basically at my feet. I had understood their weakness: they desired. And I had sensed all the destructive power provoked by this limitless desire in men. They hoped, they suffered. The most powerful sentiments. They can make you move mountains. And that power, I had it in my hands, I strung these men along, as tall, as handsome, as rich as they were. I led them where I wanted, and the worst part is that I enjoyed it. It provided me with an enormous and obscure pleasure.

The summer had slipped between our fingers like the fine sand of the beach. It would soon come to its end. Without any conclusion. Not in the affair of Niloufar, nor in that of cousin Anahid, nor in that of anyone else. The pink and the brown had definitively separated at the edge of the underwear. The sun set a little earlier each day as the circle of guests in the villa slowed. Then one day, the dreaded event took place. We realized it first through a lack, a sensorial anomaly. One morning, the villa no longer emitted the same volume of decibels as the previous days. The effervescent German cousin was no longer there. The other guests would then part in their turn, for Tehran or the other big cities in the center of the region. Once Villa Rose was without guests, Niloufar would resume her habitual solitary walks on the beach. I say "solitary," but in truth, she was never really alone. There was her dog, and, further away, the creeping shadow of her guardian angel, the silent lover, the eternal Mohamad-Réza.

When her friends were gone, and through something that resembled a bond of friendship, probably formed since our first encounter at sea, Niloufar invited me more often to Villa Rose and left the door to her bedroom open more easily. My relationship with her mother had also evolved a great deal. At the beginning, she welcomed my presence with that certain indifference possessed by people of power, those in the habit of being listened to, obeyed, and esteemed. She treated me with respect and courtesy, of course, but kept me at a distance; then, over the days, she seemed to get used to me, as one gets used to a feral cat before adopting it. She asked about me when I seemed to have been away for a while. And when I returned, she would suggest, almost out of habit, that we drink tea on the terrace. Then, inevitably, she would speak to me of my mother. That's how I found out she was born a year after my mother, that they were like sisters and had grown up together. When her father, my mother's brother, was still living in our town, my mother had lived with them for some time. It was after the death of my grandfather, when the older brother assumed the care of the orphans. No easy task, for there were four boys and three girls, of which my mother was the eldest. She even showed me a few old photos. In one, you could see the two of them on the banks of the river. They would often picnic, she told me. In the photo, there were berthed ships, an adorned tablecloth, and in the middle of the cluster of girls posing for the photograph, you could make out two young girls, around fifteen years old, both in summer dresses, with long braids that fell on either side of their shoulders. Both had their chins raised slightly, gazes directed toward a point outside the frame. Thanks to that photo, I realized that my mother had been the same height as Niloufar's mother. That she too had once been a thin and elegant young woman! Her face was as radiant and promising as that of her niece.

Strangely enough, I even found my mother to be more elegant. She already had the two vertical wrinkles between her eyebrows. To my eyes, a sign of sadness and dejection, but in the photo, they gave her a determined and willful air. She was standing behind Niloufar's mother, in a protective stance. Even though they were the same age. But one was the aunt and the other the niece. My mother never talked about that period of her life. She spoke of her early childhood, then her marriage. Her arrival in her partner's family. My birth. As if she had passed directly from little girl to spouse and mother. In the middle, something was missing. There were pages torn from her story. Now I knew which, but what did they entail? What had happened in that time? For a long time I asked myself why my mother had become my mother, and her niece, the mother of Niloufar. I would only get the answer to that question later, much later.

§

That same summer, one night in Vaveli, things almost changed once and for all. An event that could have been fatal, but that nevertheless seemed harmless to our eyes. Like a tsunami, it could have swept everything away, the competition between our suitors, my business, the circle of time, Villa Rose, and everything that constituted our feverish daily life in Chamkhaleh. It was just a few days before the unexpected departure of the German cousin.

Few people know how Vaveli was created. Even among the longtime residents of Chamkhaleh, many are unaware. They believe this place was always here. With the *"intz-intz"* of its speakers that we heard from sunset until late at night. Its youth pressed up against its door. Its love stories, its quarrels, its illusions. Its creation dates back to the years without the bridge, without electricity, at the dawn of Chamkhaleh.

At the time, when night fell, taking advantage of the veil of darkness, a man with a guitar would stand at the corner of the main avenue that led from the river to the beach and start to sing. He had an accent. He was not from the North. On this point, everyone agreed. Tall and thin, he had a funny look about him: he wore a hat that we understood later was a beret, and a three-piece suit, even though it was hot. His right foot propped on a crate of fruit, he would strum the cords of his instrument and sing. It was mainly his guitar that was the object of curiosity. Other than in movies, no one had ever seen one in real life. People would stop to listen to him, and the crowd around him grew every night. He sang popular songs and American tunes that those people didn't know at the time. It was a lot of Elvis and Dylan, we learned later. Then, one night, someone else, a guy from the area, declared himself a musician, then another. The instruments came out of nowhere. They started to play together, as a band. They had not yet given a name to this place, but Vaveli, the place that would become our headquarters, the hotbed of the summer, had just been born. The singer with the guitar ceded his place without resistance. He continued to sing a bit further away, but with far fewer spectators, and didn't come back the next summer. He didn't come back, but the place remained. People returned there, attracted by an obscure force. Each night, a crowd would form, the makeshift musicians and singers would devote themselves to their favorite pastime. Then one night, a kind of circus tent, made of a few posts covered in jute canvas, was erected and two people proclaimed themselves cashier and doorman. The musicians were set up inside. It was probably the first cabaret on the Caspian coast. And why "Vaveli"? This name that means nothing seemed so evident to us that no one questioned it. But I think I know. At that time Googoosh—oh! that diva Googoosh!—so famous in those days, on her way back from a European tour, had sung a song, which became, like all her songs, a big hit. I don't remember the title or the words, just the refrain: "*I believe, I believe, I believe, I believe . . . in love, love, love, loooove,*" she sang, shaking her head graciously with her short hair, whose style was copied by half of the women in the country. Then everyone started to repeat this refrain, only we were singing it incorrectly. We had collectively heard in the repetition of "*I believe, I believe, I believe . . .*" a succession of "Vaveli, vaveli, vaveli . . . " that no one tried to understand. No matter. Our native musicians played that song several times per night because it was so popular. We heard it from a distance. Carried on the night breeze, deformed by the poor-quality speakers and the amplifiers pushed to their limit, it confirmed once more: in Chamkhaleh, like everywhere in Iran, those words were nothing other than "Vaveli, vaveli . . . " We agreed to meet in Vaveli. We went and paid the small sum, Charon's toll, to pass through the rudimentary curtain that served as the door and enter a different world. A world whose modest decor, with its wooden benches, its hardly elevated stage in a half-circle, didn't diminish any of its magic.

At the beginning of the night, the girls would be on one side and the boys on the other. And the fathers or brothers on the right side to watch over the honor of the former. But once the night was in full force, they became so busy with other girls that that they forgot their own! Sometimes brawls broke out, a few punches were thrown, a switchblade was brandished, but it was never actually mean-spirited. Purely for show. Things quickly calmed down. The spectacle continued. The girls danced in the middle, the boys circled around them, the diameter of the second circle shrunk night after night. If vacation had lasted a bit longer, the two circles would eventually have joined. But the summer was short—and this lack of time saved the honor of the families, much more than the switchblade.

That night, the *intz-intz* of Vaveli reached us from afar. I was walking on the beach with Mohamad-Réza. The waves were unfurling at our feet. He was in a strange mood and had asked me to spend some time with him. He wanted to confide something in me. "You are my friend," he said on each occasion, with something in his voice that emphasized his sincerity. He stopped often, losing himself in the contemplation of the dark, slightly agitated sea. Bottle in hand, he was drinking Russian vodka from his father's stash. He seemed both determined and resigned, suddenly conscious that time wasn't working in his favor, tired of his role as an impassive spectator, a mistreated buffoon, the whipping boy. He couldn't take any more, he wanted to be done with it. "I'm going to ta . . . ta . . . ta . . . talk to her," he had declared, avoiding Niloufar's name. "She's going to la . . . la . . . laugh, sp . . . sp . . . spit in my face. And so what?" With those words, he had stopped, facing the sea, and was staring oddly at the waves that reflected the moon in the white line of the foam of their crests. I couldn't leave him in that state. I took him by the arm and guided him toward the village. To where the speakers were hurling at full volume: "*I believe, I believe . . .*" repeated over and over by the overworked speakers. I had to get him away from the sea, at whatever cost. He didn't want to come. He didn't care for Vaveli, like Niloufar, who never went, but he ended up giving in. Approaching the village, he emptied the bottom of the bottle in one go and followed me, staggering. I had just paid the entrance fee when I saw a blue silhouette on the other side of the curtain, an anomaly in the landscape. Then I saw cousin Anahid and the band of girls, and, in the middle of the circle, Niloufar, probably dragged there by the others. Niloufar had not noticed our arrival. I steered Mohamad-Réza to the other end of the tent, standing him in a blind spot where he couldn't see Niloufar and her friends. Many knew the talent of my stammering friend and he was often asked to sing. If he got on the stage, I could imagine what would come next . . . "If I can't manage to t . . . t . . . talk to her, then I'll ss . . . ss . . . sing." That night on the beach, he had repeated his pledge, which was already old news. And then it was the ideal moment for him. I saw him close his eyes, throw his head back, and unleash his powerful voice in a love poem by Hafez, and not just any: "No one, except my heart, in love since the dawn of time / Can labor for all eternity." I had already heard him sing it. It gave you goosebumps. "Is there a more beautiful legacy than the love song / Under the azure vault, no one knows of any." If he sang it in the presence of Niloufar, no one would be able to predict what would happen next, and that had to be avoided at all costs. My brain took one second to decide. I started to clap my hands to invite Mohamad-Réza to sing, chanting the title of one of the songs that he sang marvelously.

It was a risqué song. I was quickly joined by the others, all turned toward him. Mohamad-Réza shook his head no, but we didn't give up. It was a very difficult song to sing, because with each repetition the refrain sped up and added a stanza. It was hellish by the end, so much so that the audience couldn't follow it anymore, settled for tapping their hands and feet. It always ended in a general ruckus. Mohamad-Réza resisted for as long as he could before climbing on stage, with me almost pushing him. He then started to sing without knowing that Niloufar was in the audience. We followed the words, clapping our hands. Some, standing, tapped their feet. Mohamad-Réza let himself go with the flow. He sped up with each cycle, inviting the audience to follow him. I observed Niloufar covertly. She was stupefied, didn't imagine for an instant that Mohamad-Réza was capable of doing such a thing. Then I saw her get up and walk out the exit, no doubt outraged by the words. On the stage, microphone glued to his mouth, Mohamad-Réza, who still hadn't seen her, was drenched in sweat. He had drowned his sadness in alcohol and the levity of the moment. He was at his peak, savoring his stammerer's revenge, his audience ecstatic at his feet. Vaveli was vibrating in the summer night. He could be heard from a distance. All the way from Villa Rose, where a girl was crossing the entryway alone, her blue dress pulled by the crude hands of the night breeze. Tomorrow, another day would rise, a day similar to so many others.

In the end, Niloufar's mother wasn't all that precious. She didn't object much to speaking about her youth. All you had to do was insist, and she would close her book, put it on the table, breathe deeply, and travel back in time to recount, with a certain nostalgia, anecdotes about her aunt and friend, Fakhry. Thanks to these stories, I learned about the other side of my mother's life, I saw her other face. The more Niloufar's mother talked about those old times, the more the mystery of my mother's metamorphosis grew in my eyes. "Fakhry wasn't afraid of anything." She detested girly behavior, Niloufar's mother continued, and did everything opposite. Ran faster than the boys, fought with rage, caught snakes by the head, and, when they played hide-and-seek, she was unfindable, choosing hiding places where no one would think to go. For example, at the bottom of the old wells of the house, where she would let herself glide down the wet wall. Once at the bottom, she would lift her skirt, enter the water up to her thighs, and let the others search for her as long as she desired to remain hidden. She was happy there, in the cool, daydreaming and singing long songs that she made up herself. I said she hadn't changed in that respect. She still continued to hum those endless melodies while she was taking care of the house or the flowers in the straight paths of our garden.

The stories of Niloufar's mother strangely stopped at the moment when the two of them entered adulthood. When she got to that period, she became as evasive as my mother. I knew that these memories bothered her. I tried to figure out why. I didn't know that she herself had disappeared at that time, for a little while, before reappearing, married to the Doctor. Meanwhile, my mother had married my father, the sixth son of a rich merchant. It was the marriage that had solidified the bond between two big families of the region. I had a hunch that the answer to the enigma lay there. The gaps in the stories of their youth, the black hole of the family history had to be there. Niloufar's mother had married the young Doctor and had left to live in the big city, while my mother had remained to marry the sixth son of the merchant. An arranged marriage? Most likely. Had she been given as collateral, used as a connecting piece between two important families? Had one decided her destiny while the other had endured a choice that wasn't her own? I thought I had uncovered the secret, even if, in reality, things were much more complicated.

Parand had no chance. I knew that from the beginning. Later, when I knew Niloufar more intimately, my gut feeling changed in certainty. His Beach Boy look, his bare chest, and his mannerisms that came straight out of fashion magazines had an effect on many girls of the coast, but didn't impress Niloufar at all. No one denied that Parand was handsome. He was a very popular boy. The girls of Chamkhaleh looked for him during their nightly outings and whispered to each other as soon as he arrived. After swimming in the sea, they would pass near the volleyball net to see him, would turn around at the sound of his motorcycle, but he was unavailable, obsessed with the foreign girl. So, in common agreement and without understanding that Niloufar had nothing to do with it, they had decided she was responsible and unanimously detested her. I don't know if Niloufar had sensed this general feminine disavowal, but I'm sure that even if she had, she wouldn't have cared. How could she have? Everything that comprised poor Parand was the opposite of what held any appeal for her. In reality, he was the perfect sucker who didn't pose any threat to my business. So I let him be. Let him sink as deeply as he wanted into his farce. He had spent a good amount of his father's money stuffing me with sandwiches, or paying for my games of pool, or good hashish and everything else he could buy. It didn't work. My job was simple, maintain two base sentiments in him: desire and hope. For desire, I didn't have to do much. For hope, all I had to do was let him glimpse signs of encouragement from Niloufar. In the end, even if he gave up or walked away, it wasn't a problem. I didn't like that rich kid. I didn't know yet that soon I would carry his coffin on my shoulder and celebrate his martyrdom on the public square in front of a violent mob chanting his name, screaming for vengeance. No, I didn't know that yet, like many other things.

For Mohamad-Réza, as strange as it may seem, things were different. Niloufar was truly intrigued by him. His beaten dog expression, his nightly songs, his persistence had conquered her legendary indifference to the male sex. A woman cannot remain eternally indifferent to so much love surrendered without the expectation or hope of anything in return. Little by little, Niloufar had become used to his presence. The stammerer had become her indispensable daily companion. During her walks, when she turned around, it wasn't just to reassure herself that her dog Tamba was following her, but to verify the presence of Mohamad-Réza in the distance, beyond the dog. To see his shadow, his discreet silhouette in front of her door, the stain he made in the background of the landscape, at the top of the embankment. She had become used to falling asleep listening to his voice, and in the morning, she would discreetly poke her head out to verify that he was there, heightening the summit of the embankment with his seated half-stature. She had forbidden her friends from making fun of him, and the jokes about Mohamad-Réza had stopped. The rare times when he was absent, missing in action, she felt a strange emptiness in her heart, as if something indispensable was lacking from the order of things. On those days, during her walk, she would stop more often than usual to look for her dog in the distance. Staring at the surroundings with more attention, combing the horizon line with her gaze. Then when he came back, she would secretly celebrate his return. At night, she stayed up later than usual to listen to the melody of his melancholic songs, that voice that modulated itself, climbing and descending according to the comings and goings through the sandy paths around the villa. And so, on that morning, in her bedroom, lying on her bed, displaying that air of ennui young girls have, head tilted back, T-shirt hiked up above her magnificent golden belly button, to my great surprise, it was his name she had asked me.

"Mohamad-Réza," I had responded.

She didn't react to his old-fashioned name, she merely repeated it twice. Like a password she was trying to memorize.

Mohamad-Réza's father owned a small starch factory, Saleh Starch. You know it, I'm sure. The starch was sold in small green boxes adorned with cursive letters: "Made with the finest ingredients." I had gone to his house several times. A large, classic house. Several layers of rugs on the ground signaled the important amount of money his father earned. A heavily furnished living room, velvet armchairs and couches covered in white sheets that were used at most two or three times a year. A Russian clock with gold trim hung at the top of the stairs that led to the first floor. Silver and china sets arranged in glass armoires. And many other gilded accessories. Mohamad-Réza's mother didn't wear a veil in the house, but put on a large scarf and a long coat to go out. His sister, like all the girls her age, went to high school in uniform. At their house, no library full of books, no record player, no four o'clock tea served with caramel and chocolate, no piano in the corner of the living room, none of that. There wasn't, it seemed, any link between Mohamad-Réza's world and Niloufar's. Except perhaps money. But I knew that money held no importance in Niloufar's eyes. I had a hard time imagining her in this place. You couldn't even use the adjectives "warm" or "pleasant" for that house. And I also didn't think that the manufacturer of starch could stand up to the Doctor, not any more than my father could. No, it was impossible. On top of it all, Mohamad-Réza didn't stand out through his intellect, though he was by no means an idiot or uncultured. I imagined him having his first fight with Nilou. He would inevitably be obliged to call her by her first name, even if only one time, and would thus burn up all his ammunition with the first "ni-ni-ni" that came out of his poor mouth. No, he had no chance. And yet, it was his name that she had asked me, of all the names of the boys who swarmed around her. She was turning her head toward him. Even if I was the only one who knew, it was to him she had offered a book. She had waited for me to reach the door of her bedroom before she threw me the work, taken from the pile of books on her bedside table, and said to me with a falsely indifferent air: "Can you give this book to Mohamad-Réza?" And added, seeing my astonishment: "It can keep him company on his perch." It was a book by Nazim Hikmet, and not just any book: his love poems.

Yes, the more Parand wasn't a problem, the more Mohamad-Réza became one. Niloufar's heart decidedly remained an impenetrable mystery. She was one of those girls you couldn't say no to. The more impossible something was, the more attractive it became for her. I had guessed it. I had already seen it in her actions. She was always searching for a challenge, and if Mohamad-Réza was becoming one, there was nothing more to do.

I read and reread that book. I possessed those words, stolen three times over. Once from their poet, once more from the one to whom they had been offered, and, finally, from the one who had offered them. I never parted with the book and, if it hadn't been taken from me by force, I would have it still. I held onto it like a thief his chopped-off hand or a beggar his gold coin found in the dust.

Niloufar wasn't looking for something perfect. The world she came from was overflowing with useless perfections. In the end all that was flawed, all that fell short, benefited Mohamad-Réza in the eyes of Niloufar. Everything we consider a weakness only added to his strength. And, in this vein, he was disarming. Impossible to rival, no one could even compete. But, for all that, was he indestructible? No. No one is. He had his weaknesses. And most importantly one fatal flaw, a real fault that I was one of the few to know about. Something terrible, capable of leading to his downfall.

§

The summer was heading straight for its end. In a few days, we might have been saved by the arrival of the first autumn rains, but, that year, the clouds were slow to arrive. Summer persisted on the Caspian coast. As though destiny was at work.

The future is not constructed on the pillars of the past, but on its ruins. I drank a few more cups of tea on the terrace of Villa Rose and discovered that my mother had married the sixth son of the merchant so that Niloufar's mother could marry the Doctor and leave our little town. I was able to complete Niloufar's mother's sentences by matching them with the stories recounted by my own mother and my aunts.

One Friday, my mother's father, the stubborn mullah, the one we called "the headless sage" because of his gruff temperament and the mental lapses caused by epilepsy, the Sayyid, the self-proclaimed direct descendant of the Prophet, didn't get up from his bed. They found him dead in his bedroom, a large book open to the first page on his chest. Everyone spoke about the presence of the book to emphasize his status as a man of letters. I think that he slowly suffocated himself beneath the weight of the book, they couldn't stop talking about how hefty it was! Later, I found that famous book in our library; with its leather cover, it weighed over two pounds. It's not surprising it got the better of the old man. In any case, he was dead, and taking care of the family fell to his eldest son, the "crown prince." That's what they called my mother's eldest brother. That family was the worst inheritance one could leave a man, for, in addition to the boys, there were three girls, separated by barely a year, all approaching marriage age. Everyone knows that marrying three sisters at the same time is no small matter. My grandfather, the stubborn mullah, detached from the affairs of this world, had left nothing for their dowry and the eldest son had his own daughter to marry, his first child, his muse, the future mother of Niloufar. That's when my paternal grandfather came into the picture, a rich rice merchant who had publicly declared that one day, at whatever cost, he would take one of the Sayyid's daughters for one of his sons. Revenge, resulting from a quarrel between the two men, whose origin no one knew. The mullah, when he was alive, had always refused and had sent back the delegations who came on behalf of the merchant to ask for the hand of his daughters empty-handed, five times. He didn't consider a family of merchants worthy of the bond of marriage. On top of that, my father's father was known for being a usurer, the disgraceful occupation left in those times mainly for Jews and Armenians. But the stubborn mullah was dead, and his three daughters would soon become old hags without a dowry. What arrangement was there between the usurer and the crown prince? No one ever knew. But my mother, the eldest of the three, married the sixth son of the merchant, and the other two sisters married in their turn, bringing with them a suitable dowry.

Not long after, unburdened of his task, the crown prince left with his family to live in Rasht, the big city, capital of the region. A few years later, the niece, my mother's childhood friend, returned, accompanied by her husband, the young Doctor, to eat her first taste of my mother's buckwheat halva. She was pregnant with a girl, while my mother was struggling to have her first child. Infertile, people assumed. But how could she conceive a child when she wouldn't let the man she didn't love into her bed?

It was from Niloufar's father, alias the Doctor, that I heard politics discussed for the first time. The Doctor had two distinctive qualities. The first, I've already described: he didn't have any hair. The second, he was a communist and member of the Tudeh Party.[4] You know that at that time, the lettered—that's what we called those who had completed their studies—were divided into two groups: the supporters of Mosaddegh and the members of the Tudeh Party. The tradition in the North leaned more toward Tudeh's communism. The proximity to Russia, the legend of Mirza Koochak Khan,[5] and the Socialist Republic of Gilan[6] certainly had something to do with it. Niloufar's mother and her husband, the Doctor, were both aligned with the Tudeh Party until the 28 Mordad coup d'état,[7] the dismissal of Mosaddegh, and the dissolution of the Tudeh Party by the Shah.

After the coup d'état, the Tudeh Party, now outlawed, dissolved and its members hurried into hiding. The Doctor and his wife, originally from the North, naturally came to hide in our town. The Doctor was easily recognizable because of his scar. They said that one night, afraid of being arrested, they took off over the flooded river. They lived for some time in the Eshkevarat mountains,[8] going from village to village. One hell of an adventure; they emerged as heroes. They loved telling us about it, like a rite of passage for the family. I quickly understood why there was so much interest in these stories. For us, in the North, we idolized the courageous, those who defied taboos. We had respect for the resistance fighters, the Jangalis,[9] you know . . . the disciples of Mirza Koochak Khan. The photographs of him with a bushy beard and a gun slung over his shoulder, even though they were forbidden, could be found in many houses. Relics of a glorious and legendary past. Since then, I'd also dreamed of one day being hunted, having enemies on my trail, forging my own legend, having feats of war for people to talk about. Everything except being a man without a history and without a future, like my father. Those former Maquis, I saw them visit our area, triumphant, with their beautiful cars and their beautiful clothes, eating my mother's halva with their beautiful manners. It had paid off for them to be rebels, so it could pay off for me as well.

Mohamad-Réza was physically very strong. That's precisely where his weakness lay. And that force, which I've already described to you, was generously spread throughout all his limbs, including his genitals. You're a man, you understand what I mean. We have all felt that uncontrollable force between our legs. That autonomous muscle that wakes up first in the morning and goes to sleep last at night. That indispensable, cumbersome thing we lug around everywhere. Well, for him, it was ten times worse than for the rest of us. He possessed a penis of impressive size and his erection was a whole affair, a cramp that lasted hours, even days. Sometimes, he was even impeded by it, doubled over in a corner, incapable of getting up for fear of revealing his secret. I became aware of it, and then one day he professed its size to me in a surge of virile confidence. I knew that it happened to him on the embankment, too. At night, it was enough for a shadow to pass behind a window of the villa, with the minuscule possibility that it might be Niloufar, for his dick to straighten conspicuously, like a strange body that had been grafted onto him. And with such violence that he was in agony. He wasn't proud of it, but it was stronger than him. He couldn't fight against the urge. And so one night I went to find him with a surprise in my pocket.

§

I want you to know something: at thirteen years old, I was no longer a child, I knew what I was doing. I knew perfectly well. I had planned everything from start to finish, prepared everything in detail. I had a very precise idea of what his reaction would be. I knew that when he prowled around Villa Rose at night, he sometimes recited the Ayat al-Kursi[10] to contain his ardor. That's what the mullah had advised him. I knew that he avoided walking barefoot on Nilou's footprints in the sand, for fear it might provoke sudden ejaculation. That sometimes a sputter, a fleeting illusion, a color evoking something linked to his Nilou was enough to get him worked up. His love for Niloufar, was it all purity and poetry? I had a feeling it wasn't. All his being, all the cells comprising him were obsessed with Niloufar. How could the cells of his penis have been an exception? I knew exactly what his sexual urges could do to him. I found him at the top of the embankment. To coax him down from his watchtower, I told him that I had something for him, a very special object that was worth its weight in gold. He followed me to a quieter corner. He was hanging on my words, waiting impatiently for me to unveil this mysterious present. When I deemed him sufficiently worked up, I handed it to him. He couldn't believe his eyes. I heard him groan like a wounded animal. He was short of breath like someone who's just been stabbed in the middle of his stomach. Then I heard him say in a painful sequence of spasmodic syllables, "It's . . . it's . . . it's . . . it's Ni . . . Ni . . . Ni . . . Ni . . . ?" I nodded my head yes. He was holding Niloufar's black lace underwear in his hand and couldn't stop staring at it. He hardly dared touch it. Then, mustering up a bit of courage, he slid his fingers over the fabric that had graced her crotch and over the coarser knots of the lace, as if it were an ephemeral object, fated to disappear. His eyes followed the curves of the seams, the circular stitches of the embroidery, to the small bow sewn on the front, which would lie between the pubis and the belly button. He remained like that for a long time, squeezing the underwear in his hand, and ejaculated abundantly, even before he had a full erection.

Mohamad-Réza left, Nilou's undergarment in his hand. Later, to thank me, he showered me in presents, did me a thousand favors. I knew the power this bit of lace had on men. I was captive too. But like everything with him, it was multiplied by a thousand. From that moment on, something definitively broke in him, a barrier had been crossed. Pandora's box had opened in his brain. The genie of his outsize libido had emerged from the bottle and would never go back in. Neither the Ayat al-Kursi and its anti-erection effects, nor the talisman to calm his desire, nor any of the other *surahs* of the Quran could help him anymore. He started masturbating frantically. He did it as soon as he woke up in the morning, in bed. During the day, he hid himself in bathrooms, in an abandoned shack, behind bushes. At night, hidden in the darkness of the land around the villa. He masturbated in front of the sea after his beloved's swim. Lying in the warm sand trampled by her feet. He masturbated and masturbated again. By the end, his body could no longer produce enough sperm for his repeated ejaculations. He touched himself violently, and that violence was only heightening. Ejaculation took longer and longer to come. He couldn't control it anymore, but couldn't give up. In the end, he was exhausted. He had nothing left in his testicles, his penis was bleeding, pumped empty. It was very painful, he confided in me one day. He was withering from this excess. His skin was turning yellow, his cheeks were growing hollow, and enormous dark rings were forming under his eyes. But he continued his strange obsessive activity, haunting Villa Rose, the surrounding pathways, and the seaside village. He had been a biblical romantic, with all the despair and the delicious poetic suffering that went along with it, and I had turned him into a person possessed, a sleepwalker, a phantom, a caged beast.

Yes, my friend, I did that. Now, you might be seeing me in a different light. You can look at me with that contemptuous gaze you know so well. Yes, go ahead, look at me. Do you understand now why I came to see you? Judge me, it's your turn now. Is that not betrayal? Is it not much more despicable than all the betrayal you could have committed or imagined? I warned you, what I did is on another level. It's not a friend in arms I sent to the gallows, but a true friend. When we engage in politics, in a forbidden party, when we commit clandestine activities in a country under dictatorship, like Iran, we know the rules, more or less, right? To be denounced by a captured comrade is how it goes, isn't it? But he, Mohamad-Réza, he suspected nothing, he had signed no pact, all he had done was love, too much or too poorly perhaps, but simply loved. No matter what he became next and what he did in his turn. Now, I'm speaking about a young man, seventeen years old, madly in love, who has not yet done any harm to anyone. You're not convinced of my betrayal? Well, I'll tell you what happened next. You haven't heard anything yet.

All I had to do was wait. Mohamad-Réza would wear himself out. That fire would consume him slowly and he would soon be completely out of my way. He was already almost there. His needs were now much more urgent, he approached Villa Rose more closely than usual. Poked his head into the garden with less discretion. Niloufar's mother had noticed his persistence and had talked to me about it. Physically drained, he was even beginning to lose his best attribute. His voice. When he started to sing, his voice went higher and higher until it went off the rails. He didn't sing anymore, he howled. The young man who had had a crystalline timbre and an impressive repertoire of poems was now blaring in a broken voice and repeating the same refrains like a scratched record. We had realized it very quickly, at night, around the fire, when he started to sing without anyone asking and at inopportune moments. As soon as there was a moment of silence, he would dive into the breach and croon a few couplets, then his voice would surpass everyone else's, slide over the expanse of sand that surrounded us and muffle the sound of the waves, the cicadas, the birds. The world. We could hear only him. It was unbearable.

From that point on, he no longer sang only when necessary for dialogue. This irrepressible need to speak that animated him, that sprang forth into the most beautiful and most fitting songs, had disappeared. It had ceded its place to a simple desire to exist. He wanted to claim his presence, his unfulfilled desires. From that point on, he

screamed. His voice thundered in the night. I heard him
from my place, for I was never very far from the villa, I
too a wandering shadow. He stumbled, as at the beginning of a yawn, over certain refrains that he repeated ad
infinitum. A stabbing ritornello of sadness. Today, years
later, I still hear him, inconsolable, singing his despair to
the stars, late in the Chamkhaleh night.

The beauty of his songs had faded. Nothing remained
but the nuisance of his nocturnal racket. The mysterious silhouette we hadn't minded tolerating had become
a cumbersome presence. He was starting to agitate the
occupants of the beautiful house. All of them, except
Niloufar. Naturally, they asked me to do something about
it. Niloufar was opposed to it. She defended the singer
who had lost his way, declared that singing was in no
way obscene and that she didn't understand why we had
to put an end to it. What's more, she had said without
any intention of provocation or confrontation, but with
perhaps just a bit of insincerity, that she still found his
voice beautiful and pleasant to listen to. She had also
asked me to intervene, but in the opposite sense. As for
me, I did nothing but look after my own interests. Rather
than arranging a meeting with him as Niloufar had asked
me, or telling him to stop his serenades like her mother

asked me, I brought Mohamad-Réza another treasure, a bra. Yes, I did. I couldn't stop there. I had to stay consistent. It was the least I could do. Transgress with integrity. It was an orange bra that Niloufar often wore beneath her low-cut T-shirts and whose satin fabric straps were recognizable. Who in our entourage didn't know this piece of her lingerie? We had seen it so many times on her, how its straps cut the golden skin of her shoulders into two unequal parts. Mohamad-Réza practically snatched it out of my hand, smelled it with relish, and went off alone with it for a moment. Other pieces of lingerie followed, like booster shots. Thus, I nourished the famished beast with the intimate parcels of my cousin Niloufar. The more I gave him, the more he asked for. He was at the end of his rope. His stammering was at an all-time high. He didn't communicate anymore, practically never returned to the circle where the young boys hung out. In his eyes, I was his last friend. His sole confidante. He made the effort to speak to me, and I listened to him with patience. His words came out of his mouth one by one, reaching me in an infinite tornado. And when he couldn't find his words, he hung onto my neck to spill out torrents of tears. One day I noticed a smear of blood on his shirt. He said it was nothing, just a scratch from a night stroll, but I insisted, and he showed me the tattoo he had done on his chest with a sharp object. He showed it to me only, because I was his friend. He had carved a big "N" and then the other four letters that form "Nilou" into himself with a sharp object. A deep, oozing wound on the left side of his chest, where his lovesick heart was beating. A wound that wouldn't heal, because he picked off the scabs each morning. He wanted to literally bleed for her.

The shed was right at the foot of the wall, and its broken window offered an unobstructed view into Niloufar's bedroom. I had planned my move. One day, I told Mohamad-Réza that the window he stood in front of at night wasn't the best one. I had already located the foothold created by a cinder block protruding from the wall, the steel pole, and the edge of the framework. I brought Mohamad-Réza there one night. I showed him how to put his foot into the hole of the cinder block, grab onto the bit of metal, support himself with the pole, scale the wall, and use the roof of the shed to descend to the other side. Once over the wall, it had taken him some time to react. He was paralyzed, unable to situate himself in the night landscape. I was basically forced to place him opposite the window and to tell him, pointing my finger: "Look, down there," for him to realize that we were a few steps from Niloufar's window. The room was bathed in darkness, and the window was poorly lit.

But things gradually came into focus and we could soon make out the interior of the bedroom. The bed along the wall, the armoire, the pile of books, the door. Everything was slowly outlined as our eyes adapted to the darkness. The bedroom seemed empty. I told him to be patient. A few minutes later, the bedroom was further illuminated when a door opened. A shadow stood out more clearly. Then things became defined more sharply and, finally, we saw the contours of the window, the frame where the fatal scene would play out. We saw, as though on a movie theater screen, a spindly silhouette, with long hair and a straight back, move from left to right. There was no doubt, it was her. At the sight of Niloufar, Mohamad-Réza was so excited that I feared he would blow his load on the spot. After a few back and forths, the silhouette stopped near the window, immobile, like a cartoon on pause. We remained petrified. Despite the feeble lighting, we could finally see her up close, make out the curve of her breasts, the disorder of her hair, the contour of her hips. She seemed naked, and even though the lower part of her body wasn't visible, the darkness and our imagination took care of the rest. I remember hearing Mohamad-Réza let out a strange groan. A manifestation of pain rather than pleasure . . . He remained hunched over, in a pose of shock, biting his right index finger, completely absorbed in his contemplation, which somehow reminded me of that character often seen in Persian figurines. You must know what I'm talking about. Like figurines of Farhad, when he surprises the beautiful Shirin, naked, bathing in a fountain. Mohamad-Réza turned back toward me with a desperate look on his face. He was trembling. His eyes were misty, drowning in tears. Modesty kept him from doing anything in front of me. So I left him alone in the shed at the foot of the window, knowing that that would be his spot from then on, for all the nights to come.

After that summer, I never needed an invitation to enter the villa again. I simply pushed the door open. I had a place at the table and behaved like a member of the family. Niloufar's mother invited me to have tea or play a game of cards. Niloufar had adopted me like the brother she had never had. She confided her secrets in me more and more. I knew her taste in music, books, and her love of poetry. The walls between us seemed to be dissolving little by little, becoming thinner, more transparent. We swam together, and she taught me how to hold my breath. Even Tamba the dog had adopted me as his substitute master. He obeyed me and followed me on the beach. I hung out less often with the circle of boys, and I accepted the jibes they threw my way with a certain disdain. Our fraternal relationship suited me for the proximity it created between us, but its nature broadened our carnal distance. Niloufar behaved around me more and more like a sister, but I didn't feel like her brother. I continued to watch her discreetly. Her body flustered me if I touched her while we were swimming or when we squabbled. Sometimes she realized it and adjusted her T-shirt or pulled on the bottom of her skirt. She would ask me, when I seemed far away, daydreaming, lost in the features of her face, in the black of her eyes: "What are you looking at? What are you thinking about?" "Oh, nothing special," I would answer, trying to get a hold of myself. I had hoped that the three years' age difference between us would matter less over time. But I was wrong. She never had even the slightest amorous sentiment toward me. I had to settle for what I had, the assumed place of brother. Like Mohamad-Réza, who settled for what he had. The embankment, a few pieces of lingerie, the shed, and the window.

Mohamad-Réza was caught in the act one night. In the shed, his head through the window and his pants around his ankles. He didn't try to flee. He stayed there with his mouth agape, paralyzed, without even trying to pull his pants back up. And during all those long minutes when the Doctor smacked him with rage, he didn't lose his erection. They put him on his knees, like a torture victim, he remained immobile until the gendarmes arrived. He said nothing, keeping his head down. He started to hum a song. Which one? No one ever knew.

Niloufar saw everything from her window and cried.

I saw Niloufar cry two times. Once, when they grabbed Mohamad-Réza from her window and beat him and hand-cuffed him, and years later, when she was beaten and handcuffed in her turn. Those two times, it wasn't out of weakness, nor out of sadness, but out of rage. They say that history repeats itself twice—the second time is not necessarily as farce.

The rain arrived the day after Mohamad-Réza's arrest and, with it, the exodus of the summer vacationers from the seaside toward town. Niloufar and her family were among the first to leave. In the following days, no one among the survivors of summer lit the fire on the beach. The circle of boys disbanded and wouldn't reunite until the next summer. We knew that Mohamad-Réza had said nothing during his interrogation, not about the underwear they had found in his pocket, nor about the circumstances in which they had found him, and thus nothing about me. He had maintained a stubborn silence. The Doctor had not pressed charges, deeming that the lout had been punished enough. We didn't see Mohamad-Réza again in Chamkhaleh, nor in our town. As soon as he was released, he was sent to live with his uncle in another town for the last year of high school. He came back four years later, the day before the mass uprising that overthrew the monarchy in order to install the first Islamic Republic in history. Over the course of those four years, he had transformed into a big burly giant, practically doubled in size. His V-shaped chest and his muscular forearms were no doubt the result of long hours of physical fitness. I saw him very little. He walked with his head high, his gaze empty, his arms and thighs somewhat spread out from his body, with the gait of fighters and neighborhood thugs, indifferent to matters of the town. He didn't get back in touch with his former friends. Nor with me. He often appeared in the company of his father, whom he was helping in the starch factory. With his new attitude, he wanted to show us that he had turned the page. But, deep down, that was not at all the case.

§

I returned to Chamkhaleh not long ago. The village isn't the same anymore. Victim to its years of glory, it has swapped its soul for the riches of the city. I took the bridge that crosses the river, forced to park my car in a parking lot and walk toward the sea, and saw all the horrors of our time concentrated in one place. Where there had been cottages with straw roofs and wood bungalows, they had erected concrete to house the summer vacationers. The main dirt path that led toward the sea in times past, with strips of soft sand on the roadsides, had been paved with cracked concrete and bordered with convenience stores and small motels. The sea, whose level had risen over the past decade, inundating a good part of the coast, had withdrawn and was unfurling timidly at the edge of the beach, in its former place. I went into the village, which now resembled a marshaling yard to divide up the tourists by category and herd them toward the hotels, the guest rooms, and the seasonal rental bungalows. I turned around and took one of the side roads to the right. I was able to find my way through the labyrinth of redesigned streets and eventually recognized Villa Rose. Still facing the sea, but hidden by a man-made hill that had been erected to cut off its view. The villa, though a bit faded, had kept its pink tint. It was the off-season and empty, like many houses. I walked along the wall. Behind the villa, I found the low wall with the cinder block, the electric pole that adjoined it and, higher up, the bit of framework coming out of the concrete that had served as a handle. I hadn't forgotten any of these steps. I scaled the wall without too much difficulty. From the other side, the small shed was calmly in its place. Its roof squeaked a bit more beneath my fifty years, and I slid down its slope to land in the garden. The bedroom window had been closed off with wooden slats. The terrace was covered in sand and dead leaves. Ivy and other wild plants were growing in the cracks of the walls and between the tiles. The balcony chairs were all rusted, and the surface of the table was warped. Where would Nilou's mother put her cup of tea and her book if she decided to live here again? I did a tour of the house. All the doors and windows were locked from the inside. All except for one door that appeared to be ill-fitting in its frame. I was able to push it open without too much difficulty. The villa seemed to have been used as a squat. Floor littered with plastic bottles, wrappers, and food scraps. A few improvised beds here and there. A hangout for junkies? Perhaps. Niloufar's bedroom wasn't any better. The bed had been broken and shoved in a corner. The blue dress was missing from the gutted armoire. All the objects of value had been taken. I started to search. I didn't know what for exactly, but something that might have eluded the pillaging. A pillaging I had contributed to in my own way, as small as it might have been. That thing must have been somewhere. A sign of the time that had passed between these walls. A memory of those burned years. Even if only just a pin, a button wedged in a parquet floor groove, a bit of seashell collected by Niloufar during one of her long dives underwater. But no, nothing. Just the snickering ruins of the past. The vestiges of our wasted lives.

Through the window and the cracked glass, the song of the sea flooded into the bedroom. With time, the hill erected opposite the open sea had flattened, returning to the villa a portion of its beautiful view of the waves. Through the other window, I saw the small shed, still standing, with its wooden door and its tragic window.

During the school year, for every vacation, I always went to Rasht, where Niloufar lived with her family. As with Villa Rose, their door remained open to me. The Doctor welcomed me gracefully, no doubt for the trusted favor I had done him. When it came to memories of the summer, we avoided mentioning the incident with Mohamad-Réza. An excessive caution that showed Niloufar was still very affected by it. During my trips to their house, I spent the majority of my time with her. Her father was often absent, and her mother very busy with her role as a modern woman of high society. She was the volunteer director or member of several charitable organizations. Abandoned by her two parents, Niloufar was responsible for her own life. In this respect, she was very different from other girls her age. Her time, her mind, and her body were free. She could just as easily wear her father's pants, floating in them, as an extremely short skirt, for every head to turn as she passed. Behavior like that was admissible in Chamkhaleh, but here, in town, it was another story. She was unclassifiable, evolved within boundaries unique to her. So, sometimes they called her a tease, sometimes a tomboy. Some even called her "Monsieur Niloufar." She seemed to laugh it off. But was she really laughing? I don't think so. That's what she wanted people to think. That she not only accepted this role, but delighted in it. Playing the girl who's not faint-hearted and won't hesitate to be provocative about any subject. In truth it was nothing but a facade. It secretly pained her to be considered a rich kid, even when she walked around barefoot or dressed like a beggar. She was irremediably the spoiled daughter of her "Doctor daddy." That's how it always is. We show what we want to hide the most. She hated her condition, but couldn't strip herself of it, like a birthmark. Later on, she would pay for all those things very dearly. When the country was handed over to shortsighted monsters from beyond the grave. In the times to come, when she would no longer be protected by her father's name nor by the great lineage and elegance of her mother, Niloufar would have to accept being what she hated most, what she had fought against her entire life. A spoiled girl, a rich kid, rejected and exiled.

Despite my repeated trips to their home, I could never get used to the splendor of their life. To the logic of their existence. Their house was so big that I continued to discover new nooks at every visit. Each time was like the first time. Like Anahid, the German cousin, I was rediscovering everything. The library full of books. The piano on which Niloufar played songs at her mother's insistence. The maid who served tea and lemonade without anyone asking for it. Their English garden. Their beautiful car and the chauffeur always available to take them wherever they wanted. I was forever amazed by the finesse of the furniture, the delicacy of the decoration. In the rooms Niloufar moved through with disdain, even disgust, I slowed my pace to drink up the beauty. Niloufar's mother smelled good, with her long fingers and her perfectly polished nails, while my mother's hands were ruined by household tasks. My mother and her dress with the loud floral pattern, her flab spilling out along with the odors of our next meal. I couldn't stop myself from comparing. The Doctor spoke and shared his opinions with confidence, while my father blushed at each phrase and tripped over apologies. The Doctor sat with his chest straight and his legs spread, while my father was always bent over himself, like a crumpled ball of paper. I can still see Niloufar's mother crossing the great vestibule, then the terrace, in one of her long dresses, à la Greta Garbo, that hugged her svelte body marvelously. Smiling. Watching her, I could never get enough. The more time I spent there, the more I got used to it and the harder it became to return to our "warm little house." After each trip, my attitude changed a bit more. I was ungracious and contemptuous toward my parents. My mother noticed, but said nothing. She retaliated in her own way. With an excellent stuffed eggplant or another of my favorite dishes. One day she told me that I shouldn't judge by appearances, that people's lives aren't only what we see of them. She was right. She knew things, my mother. I learned later that Niloufar's parents hated each other and had been violently ripping each other to shreds for years through their lawyers. Not long after Niloufar's birth, the couple had started sleeping in separate bedrooms. The Doctor had numerous mistresses and was leading a double life. He ate alone in the kitchen, without even sitting down, then shut himself in his bedroom for the night. I didn't understand the gravity of those things. How can one be unhappy when they have such a luxurious lifestyle? What is certain is that Niloufar and I weren't in the right places, as if we had been born into the wrong families. Niloufar detested her mother's social life, hated her coldness and her distance. As for her father, she took for arrogance what I understood as confidence. She hated that enormous house, the over-tended gardens, the chef's refined dishes. She had been the first to call our house "warm," an adjective that had been adopted by the others. Now I understood those few extra seconds she lingered in my mother's arms, nestled against her curves. The joy on her face when she smelled the simple flowers in our garden, climbing and descending our meager stone staircase lacking in symmetry or aesthetics. She even appreciated my father for his modesty and his simplicity, for his honesty, which was, nonetheless, so harmful to our daily life. Yes, decidedly, life makes no sense.

§

The next summer arrived in the order of the seasons, and the fire on the beach was relit like the semaphore of our youth. Parand reappeared with a new motorcycle that was even bigger and shinier than the previous one. The passing of hashish recommenced, as did the bottles of beer in the plastic bucket, the salacious jokes, and the stories about girls. At that age, a year isn't enough time to grow up.

During the winter, they built the bridge over the river. The village was no longer an enclave, and the tourists from Tehran had started to flock to that part of the coast, until then spared. Their arrival en masse changed the order of things in many ways. The general ambiance, of course, but also the mix of populations. Everything transformed brutally. For us, the hunting ground remained intact, but the number of prey had heightened considerably. It was the general consensus that it was easier to seal the deal with the visiting girls than with those from our region. This view motivated my friends, and consequently everyone thought they had much more bread on their plate.

Around the fire, the stammerer was missing in action, and no one asked about him. Even his aunt's house, where he had spent his summer vacations, had remained unoccupied that year. For him, the Chamkhaleh chapter was closed. The page had been turned. Our summer festivities picked back up without anyone worrying about the empty spot on the embankment, the disappearance of his lyrical flights in the night. No one, except perhaps Niloufar, who, every morning, threw a fortuitous look in the direction of the hill, where something was missing. Her walks on the beach became more languid, her steps slower. The sounds emanating from the villa dropped a few decibels. All of this was invisible to the eyes of others, and the summer unfolded as if nothing had happened the year before, as if the tragedy of Mohamad-Réza had been nothing but another anecdote written on the ephemeral page of the sand. Was it that, or was everyone pretending they hadn't noticed? Like a collective guilt that everyone was trying to suppress. But how had Mohamad-Réza been caught? No one knew. No one, apart from me and the Doctor. I had, in fact, revealed Mohamad-Réza's secret to the Doctor. The time and regularity of his passages, his hiding spot. I had revealed all the useful details to him, praising myself for doing the right thing, but obviously not able to take part openly in the affair. He had taken my word for it. That night, when Mohamad-Réza scaled the wall of the villa, unlike the other nights, he was expected. The Doctor had organized everything without telling his daughter. Did he fear some complicity between Niloufar and Mohamad-Réza? It was very possible. Clubs had been brought in case the intruder resisted. The chauffeur had even brought his cousin as backup, a big burly guy with a reputation for being brutal, someone you don't want to cross.

I wasn't far, hidden in a corner like a despicable Judas. I saw everything from my hiding place. I, the architect of misfortune. I heard everything. The strikes, the song he was humming, Niloufar's sobs. When they took him away, hobbling because of his lowered pants, they passed near me. In the gleam of headlights from the gendarme's Jeep that had come to grab Mohamad-Réza, I could see his folded body, his swollen face, and especially his eyes. They were empty. There was nothing behind his eyelids. A face without a gaze.

Mohamad-Réza had everything stacked against him. The underwear found in his pocket and sprinkled on the terrace as pieces of evidence, the footprints on the roof of the shed, the sperm stains on the floor and everywhere else. And he endured it all. The shattered love, the shame, the face of his beloved, stunned at the window. It was predictable. He acted exactly how I had imagined. The catastrophe had taken place, but it wasn't pleasant to watch. Mohamad-Réza was henceforth stricken from Niloufar's life for good, and as a result, from mine. I was convinced of it. I thought I would never again cross paths with him, hear his voice or his stammering, but I was wrong.

So you see, my friend, the domain of evil is far vaster than that of good. Much more complex, much deeper. Evil has more feathers in its cap, infinitely more tricks up its sleeve. You thought you had behaved badly. You cried your shame into my arms for nights on end. What you did doesn't at all compare to the misfortune I caused. That man you confided in, who you admired for his supposed courage and his legendary resistance, who you wanted to resemble, as you told me a thousand times, was nothing more than a bastard. There we go, that's better. It's that look of contempt that I need. Horror, disgust, abomination, spit in my face. Not from just anyone, but from you. If I need to be judged by someone, it's you. If I have to be thrown outside, let it be by you. Better late than never.

§

Other summers went by without any major event.

Then the people of Iran rose up. But why? For what reason did the people take to the streets to demand the Shah's departure? I assure you that if we asked the question today, the majority of Iranians wouldn't know how to respond. For liberty? I don't think so. For a better life? I don't think that's it either. Because, starting in 1979, they have been far less free, their lives more difficult than before, and yet they don't rise up. So why was this country handed over to mullahs? In exchange for what? No one knows. It's strange how in a society revolt can suddenly become a necessity. And to be revolutionary, a virtue. In the summer of 1978, around the fire, we had emptied the last bottles of our local Shams beer and gulped the last drops of our artisanal arak as we watched the Caspian unfurl over the golden sand. In the few years, since the construction of the bridge, Chamkhaleh had become a prime tourist destination. Solid houses had replaced bungalows and cottages. The roads, no longer dirt paths, were now illuminated, and the chess games between boys and girls in the darkness of the night had fallen into oblivion. We no longer went out as families on the strip of sand, formerly the place of our romantic summer rendezvous, for access to the mouth of the river had been closed off by the walls of a newly constructed hotel complex. Of course, Vaveli still existed, but its magic had disappeared ages ago. It now had high walls, a powerful sound system, and comfortable chairs. A bouncer at the door now asked for an exorbitant sum, and the natives had deserted it. This campfire burning on the beach was the last one, it would soon go out and, without this semaphore, the circle of boys would forever disband. Parand, unaware of the bullet that would strike his heart in the near future, was still showboating. He was more convinced than ever of his chances with Niloufar and was determined to seal the deal before the end of the summer. Mostafa, whose body would soon be torn to shreds by shrapnel, was improvising another song, which would be his last. Ahmad, who would be decapitated in the explosion of his tank, was pulling frantically on the hashish pipe. Behnam, who would hang himself one night from the tree in his garden, still had his wit and was telling a simple story with enthusiasm. Those around the fire would all perish, each in his own way. Our generation would be decimated. If we were to have a reunion one day, it would have to take place in a cemetery. A chasm would open beneath our feet from one moment to the next and cut the summer short, offering the ultimate excuse to Parand for not having clinched his unreciprocated love. Unwavering, he told us to meet him the next summer, always just as sure of himself, but there was no next summer. There wouldn't be another summer for a long time. You remember . . .

I'm the one who gave those first books to Niloufar. *Nana* by Zola, *The Enchanted Soul* by Romain Rolland, *Mother* by Gorky, *The Quiet Don* by Sholokhov, *The Seed Beneath the Snow* by Silone. These were the classics of what we called anti-system literature. Niloufar devoured them avidly and talked to me about them passionately. I read a bit of everything. Anything that was considered subversive.

In my readings, the religious thinkers rubbed shoulders with the Marxist theorists, the humanists frequented the Stalinist determinists. By blending them as best I could, I created my own mixture and enlivened my nights with Niloufar. That modest progress was enough for me to become something of a spiritual guide for her, a mentor. I had quickly understood: in her relentless fight against her circumstances, Niloufar needed an intellectual arsenal. In her eyes, her parents were nothing but traitors to the cause, sellouts. She thought she'd be able to find the proof in the books I was secretly giving her. Those same books that her parents had surely also read and whose precepts they knew, but which, in an act of political treason, they had stopped believing, Niloufar said.

Those ideas gleaned here and there, I put them end to end, as one builds a Meccano set, to formulate a system of thought to test on others. It worked pretty well. Little by little, I forged myself a reputation as a subversive thinker, formidable and feared. Bullshit! I understood nothing of my own gibberish. But it didn't matter. The important thing was being able to maintain a line of thought. Fabricate a supposed idea that was out of the ordinary. And I did that. I had a good memory, and I had a gift: my formidable power of conviction. Already, at thirteen years old, I was capable of proving something and, later on, its opposite, without being caught in the contradiction. And while being profoundly sincere each time. Conviction is a virus that you carry inside you and that you can use to inoculate others. It's a magical thing, which people need and lack. I understood that very early on. It was a gift I was polishing in secret, like a weapon, and that, like all gifts, could turn out to be a curse. A weapon that, like all weapons, could one day come back to hurt its inventor. But this was the moment, the coveted opportunity to use it to my advantage. I possessed knowledge that the others around me didn't. Thus, I held the power. Again, that magic word, "power." Because of that, I was treated with respect. I had finally had a taste of the pleasure of politics. Even if at the time we didn't really consider it as being political. It was something else for us. More of an ideal. A reason to be a mystic, romantic, and revolutionary at the same time. I thought I had begun a career that a few years later would procure me a social rank similar to that of the Doctor. I was convinced that I could even do much better than the Doctor and his friends. I had a head start and had learned from their failure. I was set to become a powerful and prosperous man like him, with hair on top of it. In those times, the power of the shah still seemed solid. There was the famous secret police, the SAVAK, who seemed to have ears everywhere. They might have heard everything, but they certainly didn't understand much! We learned that later, when everything crumbled like a house of cards. You lived through those years, you know what I'm talking about. Under the Shah's dictatorship, being a revolutionary was as easy as being a counterrevolutionary under Pol Pot. To be labeled as such, a professor had only to propose a subject that was slightly different or a book that was a bit unusual to his students. I understood. I refined the machine. I was crafty. I had the skill to walk the line between the licit and the illicit. Between the tolerated and the forbidden. Despite the popular belief, the Shah's regime was more tolerant than that of the mullahs. An edifying example was the case of the Doctor, of Niloufar's mother, and people of their generation. They were declared enemies of the Shah's regime, even joined the resistance, but, once politics were put aside, they were able to become doctors, mayors, or congressmen. Because the Shah's police were concerned with what you did or said, but not with your thoughts. The Islamic Regime goes after what you think. Not what you've done, but what you're likely to do.

I have to tell you right away that the "Grand Soir," the "Homme Nouveau" and the Socialist International were not at all my cup of tea. I didn't care about them at all. I was seeking something else. I was following a path that had been marked for me, my own destiny. During my nights with Niloufar, I didn't care about progress or the future of humanity, I sought only her proximity. I wanted her to see me in a new light, to treat me differently. And I had obtained what I wanted. She was finally mine. Though I didn't have her body, I had her soul.

The Doctor sometimes regarded my comings and goings with suspicion, wondering what I was scheming with his daughter, but her mother seemed rather content. She believed that, thanks to me, her daughter was finally walking in her footsteps. She even contributed, furthermore, by unearthing the books of the Tudeh Party she had kept, mostly Russian literature, translated into Persian by Behazin, the appointed translator of the organization. She secretly slipped these books to me for her daughter to read, thinking Niloufar would accept them more readily from me. One day, she had entrusted one of them to me as if she were putting a time bomb in my hands. It was Lenin's *What Is to Be Done?* It was a show of trust, a priceless present to her eyes. I read the three hundred pages several times, written in microscopic letters, but I didn't really understand anything. The internal debates between Lenin, whose name I already knew, and Bukharin, who I knew nothing about, were so abstruse, so opaque, that I couldn't even pull anything from them to flaunt in front of my disciples. It was disappointing. But it was in my repertoire, arranged next to the love poems of Nazim Hikmet, like a secret tunnel toward the inexpressible. Except that with the poems of Nazim, I understood absolutely every word. I drank up every syllable. I read them on a loop, like secret seances of mental flagellation. Knowing deep down that I was incapable of living them. For me, everything was more complex. The road that led to love was long and tortuous. My words from the heart had to be soaked in blood and pain. I couldn't do anything simply.

The Doctor had turned the page long ago. At least that's what he thought. Later he would learn that, in the eyes of others, a member of the Tudeh Party always remained a member of the Tudeh Party, even if he became king one day. But, at that time, he was still busy with his important friends, occupied by his games of backgammon, his mayoral mandates, his medical practice, and his mistresses. For Niloufar's mother, it was different. She was following the rumors of revolt that were spreading in the four corners of the country and sweeping through the regions like a brush fire. She was probing the air, scrutinizing the flow of water. She would listen to Radio Moscow and Persian BBC every night, in the hope of finally finding the proof of her victory over her eternal enemies: world imperialism, the shah's regime, and their undercover agent, her husband, the Doctor.

Under the republic of mullahs, the Doctor spent two years of his life in the horrific Rasht prison. In addition to his links with the former regime, he was accused of having helped and cultivated underground activists—something he did do and didn't deny. When he was let out of prison, he was banned from the medical profession. He ended up dying in the home of one of his mistresses, who had welcomed him purely out of pity, ruined, sick, and crushed by too much opium.

§

The groans rumbling in the background started to turn into a real uproar, a prophetic sign of an enormous earthquake that would bring back the old country. The ancient kingdom. The students of the universities in Tehran protested openly. The clashes with the police multiplied, under any pretext, sometimes even for no apparent reason. My semi-clandestine activism was in full swing. I grew a nice leftist mustache. I had square-frame glasses and a strategically worn gray vest. People were fighting to participate in the covert gatherings we organized regularly, whose cadence heightened as the social climate heated up. "Clandestine" was a rather grand word. We had to really push our naivety to think they were. We were infiltrated down to the bone. Reports on our notorious gatherings were written up by several people and scattered on the desk of the chief investigator before we had even returned to our homes. Reports that, later, the chief of police would brandish, cackling, before my eyes. In the summer of 1978, Cinema Rex in Abadan caught fire. More than four hundred people died there, burned alive. All evidence suggested arson. Accusatory fingers pointed to the Shah and his secret police. Unanimously, you remember? No matter what side you were on. It was the fatal blow. The spark in the powder kegs. Charred bodies were shown in photos that circulated in secret. The Shah's regime couldn't recover from that.

What an enormous lie! What a tour de force! Who can still deny today that the cinema was set on fire by Muslim activists, following a fatwa issued by an ayatollah? What interest did the Shah's regime have in setting fire to a cinema in a working-class neighborhood of a second-tier city? Really, what interest? But in that moment, in this country of nearly forty million inhabitants, no one was lucid enough to ask that simple question and denounce the absurdity of the idea. We had all taken part in this lie. That very day, I wrote a few incensed lines, bloated with spiteful sentimentality, against the presumed assassins, who I called poodles of American imperialism, lines copied that very night by the members of our circle and distributed throughout the city. The impact was guaranteed. A revolution whose instigators are individuals like me cannot engender anything better than the monsters it birthed. A few days later, a spontaneous protest took place in the center of town. We chanted "Killer King!" with conviction. A police officer panicked. A bullet was shot, ricocheted somewhere and struck Parand's chest. What was he doing there, that rich kid? What skirt had he come to chase in this part of the street? Who knows. That said, Parand was the perfect martyr, young and handsome enough to become an icon, with a powerful father and a large family. Just the members of his family alone were enough people to start a revolution in a small European country. Considered by his family to be his best friend and perhaps the most dignified of the group, I became the organizer of his funeral services and also the guardian of his martyrdom. I'm the one who made all the decisions. The hour and the place of the transport of his body, the itinerary of the funerary procession, the slogans, the chants, the music, everything. It was grandiose. I carried his coffin myself, and I spoke on the public square to the bereaved crowd. I denounced that odious crime. I spoke of Parand, his generosity, his propriety, his simplicity, and his loyalty, his youth destroyed for capital's continued reign. Yes, I said "capital," but I don't think anyone understood what I meant. They imagined the worst, something very, very bad. At the end of the ceremony, his father took me in his arms and publicly declared that from then on I would be like a son to him and he would watch over me like his prized possession. Many cried; I wiped away a tear.

It was the beginning of the summer, but no one was thinking anymore about the sea, summer flings, or other vacation trifles. That year, the summer exodus to Chamkhaleh didn't happen. A few families made the move, but the majority remained in the city. The spirit of the summer was dead. The floodgates were open. Chamkhaleh would surrender without a fight, and without even knowing. Finished. Even if we blew up the bridge, even if we dug another river, it wouldn't help, nothing would protect it, for, like for the other towns, Chamkhaleh would be defeated from within. Those who were supposed to defend it were now gravediggers. No one dreamed of relighting the fire on the beach, of singing at night, stringing up the volleyball net, mooring the boats, nor of a thousand other things. Villa Rose remained empty. Its windows dark and its terrace lifeless. That page had been turned in the memory of the Caspian. The end was already here. We couldn't have seen it coming, that sad end, as busy as we were destroying our world.

My career had officially been launched. Parand's blood had supplied the fuel, the collective ignorance the base, the brandished fists and the mass fervor the vehicle. My path seemed clear. I would be propelled to the summit, but not exactly the one I was hoping for. I was wrong on one point, a significant one. It wasn't us who would kiss the victory cup and take power. The history of the Tudeh Party wouldn't repeat itself. An entirely different destiny awaited me. I know now that every population creates its lies. Lies have no sides, no defined color, they're not anyone's monopoly. To devise an ideology, a religion, a revolution, you also have to fashion lies to go along with it. The higher you go in the spheres, the more the taboo of lying dissipates. Its meaning and its substance transforms. Up high, they don't debate anymore what is true or false. Truths and non-truths alike are made up by them. I am convinced that even the grand ayatollahs, the cardinals, even the pope, once at that level, stop believing in God. Just as the bigwigs, so-called socialists or communists, no longer believe in the myth of social equality. I understood all of that very quickly. Perhaps faster than many others. Certainly faster than you. That's why you were able to keep your faith, your innocence, and I wasn't. When you fought for your ideas, which you believed were vital, life-saving, and just, others like me were busy making them up. And I fabricated them in my own way. I came up with my own ideas first, then the ideas that were useful to me. I'm not saying there's no real conviction, no real desire to do good, I'm just saying that the higher you climb, the rarer it becomes. I know. I was at the summit.

Cyrus came to find me one day. He had heard of my exploits. Officially, he was a student, originally from our city, studying at the University of Tehran. A chubby young man, not very tall, who blushed at every hint of emotion in his conversations, far from the prototypical underground activist. However, he's the one who introduced me to the organizations and the schools of thought in Tehran. I don't know how we decided to meet for the first time in Chamkhaleh. Perhaps because it was the off season and his family had a villa that could serve as a secure loca-tion. For some mysterious reason, Chamkhaleh would remain a part of my destiny. It was winter. The seaside was almost empty, sad and somber, as cities can be with-out their inhabitants. The sky was low, the sea black and agitated. The bad weather had destroyed the soft face of the coastline by digging crevasses and savage streams. The meeting place wasn't far from Villa Rose. I felt like a criminal returning to the scene of the crime. Everything reminded me of the stories of previous summers. The phantom of Mohamad-Réza haunted the wet sand of the deserted roads. Gusts of wind brought back the notes of a plaintive song audible to only my ears. Someone was bemoaning a lost love, a squandered passion. I sat with my back to the window so I wouldn't see Villa Rose, the sea, and the phantom silhouette.

Shut in the house, we spoke for hours and hours. Cyrus was trying to convince me of the necessity of joining an organization, in particular the organization for which he was campaigning. It was a movement that had active members in Tehran, in the big universities, and maintained links with Iranian students abroad. I retorted that a local anchor was always more efficient, less vulnerable to police attack. He advanced the necessity of a more general workers' movement, a party, the new revolutionary communist party. I didn't let myself be taken in. I said that a party of that caliber wasn't something to be created by leftist intellectuals, that it would only result in a territorial struggle. I was devilishly convincing, at the peak of my craft, and Cyrus found himself lacking in arguments to convert me. In the end, he took a book out of his bag and handed it to me as if he were brandishing a winning card. He suggested I read it before our next meeting. I immediately recognized the work. It was a new edition of *What Is to Be Done?* by Lenin. I looked at it with a certain condescension, finally understanding how that book would be of use to me. I told him he could keep it or give it to someone else. I already had the original edition.

We left Chamkhaleh again and went our separate ways just after the bridge. He seemed firmly to believe that he had made progress in the recruitment of a high-value member, and I was certain I had succeeded in hoisting my personal enterprise to a national level.

Cyrus would be my representative in the high spheres, and my reputation or, more accurately, my personal life, would take on another dimension. For the moment, I existed fully in and beyond our small region. All I had to do was let the others do the work for me. They would peddle the news that I just had to half-heartedly refute or vaguely shirk. They would try to hide the relationship they had with me and, in doing so, would identify me more than ever. It was thrilling. All I had to do was be arrested, imprisoned for just a short amount of time, for something small, but just big enough, and things would be perfect. I would obtain what I wanted, the doors of numerous houses would open to me, I would be loved and idolized by the others, and among the others of course were women. I had plenty of proof that my status as an underground activist had a powerful allure over them. Women like to offer themselves to exceptional men. Courage and intelligence attracts them. That charm worked on many of them, but not on Niloufar. In any event, not as I had hoped. Niloufar was unlike any other woman.

One day, I asked Niloufar's mother if she had other books by Lenin or other similar works. She told me yes, then had me walk up a floor. The large house had numerous unoccupied rooms. She opened a door and behind it I found what I saw as absolute power. It was a large room that was dark but well ventilated. It was practically empty and, for that reason, the wooden boxes, filled with books, stored at the foot of the walls, captured all my attention. I started by taking a few out to read the title and the name of the author. I didn't recognize any of them, but I knew intuitively that I was standing before a real treasure trove. Niloufar's mother leaned over my shoulder and looked with me, as if she herself were seeing these books for the first time. Then I heard her say in a barely audible voice: "It's the party's regional library." And she added with her customary contempt: "You know, the translation and publication branch was very active." When she said "the party," she meant the Tudeh Party. Naturally. I had never seen so many books in the same place. "They have a strange odor, don't you think?" she added with a hint of mischief in her voice. She was right; in addition to the odor of ink and old paper, the books emanated a scent I couldn't identify. Then she left me alone with the books, but, before she left the room, she turned back toward me to say: "Remind me to tell you their backstory. You'll see, it's incredible." And she told me their backstory that very night. In a lowered voice, as if we were surrounded by eavesdropping ears. "The walls have mice, and the mice have ears!"

After the dissolution of the Tudeh Party, it was no longer possible to keep these books. They had to disappear and, as the director of the regional library, that difficult task fell to Niloufar's mother. She had taken them one night to burn in a field. As you know, we have a track record of burning or burying books in this country. Our history still bears the dark traces. But she was never able to complete the task. "They were like my children," she said to me, sighing in her armchair. "Burning a book is like burning a person." So she had brought them to one of her uncles, who is also my uncle, a rice merchant. He had large warehouses, and she hoped to find a place to hide them there. But her uncle had refused. Too risky, he had declared. That's when she'd had a stroke of genius. She bought an entire truckload of rice. She and a few friends removed some of the rice from each sack and replaced it with a few books. The sacks of rice stuffed with books were all placed in a truck. Then she sent the cargo to the other side of the country. The person who received the cargo, a member of the party or another trusted person, in on the plan, made up a problem, the quality of the merchandise or its elevated price, and sent the cargo back to the sender. And the operation would repeat, headed for another destination. Thus the party's books crisscrossed the entire country several times, until things calmed down. The police pressure dissipated, and the books ended up in these wooden boxes, safe and sound, in the Doctor's house. Hence the strange odor they emitted. The odor of rice.

§

I was finally arrested in the winter of 1978, a month before the shah's departure. Four men dressed in plain clothes showed up at my house. They rifled through my things, read the scraps of paper they found here and there, and took me, me and a few of my books that had been deemed suspect. My parents remained silent. My father just shook his head when I passed in front of him, as if to say "You asked for it." Everything unfurled in perfect silence. No handcuffs. The neighbors noticed nothing. My parents listened scrupulously to the police advice and didn't speak to anyone. I was freed a few days later. I followed the same instructions. I didn't speak to anyone about the arrest. But it didn't matter, because everyone knew. Including Niloufar.

Soon after, Cyrus got back in contact with me. He wanted to meet again: this time, he wanted to bring along a member of the delegation. He didn't say anything more. I knew that he couldn't and that I shouldn't ask any more questions. I assumed a "member" had to be someone important. I suggested we meet in Rasht and I asked Niloufar if we could use their house for the meeting. I remained very vague about who would be there. Niloufar welcomed my demand with a certain enthusiasm. She must have found it exciting. She took care of the arrangements, chose a day when her parents would both be away, dismissed the servants, and cleared out the place so the meeting could go as planned. She even kept watch from the window and surveilled the street to guarantee our security. That day, Cyrus came accompanied by a man who was about forty years old, balding, and wearing round-framed glasses. They moved through the splendor of the house without making any remark, almost too rapidly for it to be natural. I knew that wealth always had an effect on people, no matter what side they were on. We sat around the walnut table in the living room. They questioned me again, asked me my opinion on things. The man with the round-framed glasses seemed interested in my responses. He noted everything in small handwriting on cigarette papers, all while displaying a slightly dubious air, somewhere between astonishment and stupor. He was surely someone important in the hierarchy of the organization. I had been successful once more. In the end, he seemed won over and acquiesced to the majority of my proposals.

The meeting lasted three hours. Then they left, one after the other, in five-minute intervals. The exchanges we had bore no importance. If you asked me what was said that day, I wouldn't be able to remember anything in the slightest. What mattered was that it happened in the Doctor's home. Before Niloufar's eyes. What mattered is that she was at the window, signaling to me that everything was okay, that I too could leave safely. It was the expression in her eyes, which I interpreted as admiration. It was the first of a series of meetings we would have in that house.

The books were arranged by theme. World history, religious history, antique Persian history. Then political books, many by Marx, their white covers stamped with his hairy effigy. *Capital, Outlines of a Critique of Political Economy, Anti-Dühring, Critique of Hegel's "Philosophy of Right."* Then Lenin's works. Then philosophy and literature, in particular Russian literature, which I read avidly and hungrily. And the more I read, the more I realized that the key to power was there, buried like grains of rice in the twists and turns of the books that were sleeping in those wooden boxes. I put my memorization capabilities to full use. At that age, my head was like a big empty hard drive, capable of storing tons of megabytes that I registered and reproduced, adding my own personal touch, my knowledge, during meetings and debates that we organized in secret. That's how I became the king of the mythmakers. "Mythmaker" is the least denigrating adjective that I can use to describe myself. In my head, I developed a strange machine capable of developing all sorts of ideas, theories, and arguments. I was able to grab hold of absolutely any idea and to erect a heap of things around it. Weave a web dense and solid enough to confound anyone. Except, knowledge without engagement is the worst thing. And even if my power was linked to the lack of education within my entourage, it was still power. How could I not revel in it? How could someone ask a powerful person not to? My notoriety extended even into my own family. I was able to talk, knowing that they were listening to me attentively. When I felt that delight, I put my powerful instrument of mythmaking into action. I remember that at the peak of my craft, when we were gathered as a family in the respectful silence of the group listening to me, I turned toward my father to see if he finally felt avenged for his silence, for the contempt I knew he felt, through the eloquence of his prodigal son. But, each time, I noticed with astonishment that my father was the only one who wasn't listening to me. He was, as always, red with shame, secretly suffering per usual. One day, he confessed to me just how much he hated my soliloquies, my erudite tirades, my speeches. He found me vulgar, boastful, and dishonest. He said that I was the failure of his life and that he bitterly regretted not having passed down to me even a bit of abnegation, good sense, and honesty, values indispensable to being a good man, in his eyes. He was right about that. He saw things as they were, my poor father!

The protests were happening more and more frequently, do you remember? With each protest, there were one or two deaths, those fallen under the bullets of the Shah's army. Their burials broke out into riots and there were more deaths, and so on, like a vicious cycle. 17 Shahrivar 1357,[11] the soldiers shot into the crowd of a big protest.

"Four thousand dead on Jaleh Square!" Four thousand, they said! Can you imagine? The bigger the lie, the better it takes. How many died that day? How many really? Eighty? A hundred, at the absolute maximum. I don't want to cling to macabre numbers. A crime is a crime, and even the death of one innocent person is intolerable. But okay, it was one more lie in the terrible machination of the 1979 Revolution. And once again, we all took part in that lie. We had all relayed it, without making any effort to verify the information. For all of us, the most important thing was the fall of the shah. A puppet of imperialism, according to us, the people of the left, an infidel enemy of Islam, according to the religious. We know now that it was neither one nor the other. Death to the king! That was our only slogan. Every fist raised for that. Every mouth repeated it. And the shah left. It was the second time that his people had forced him out. The first time, as you know, he left in 1953, and returned after the famous American coup d'état, incited by CIA agents who were aided by spies, the bribed crooks from the slums, and prostitutes. And with the complicity of the Tudeh Party, which didn't stop them from being among the victims of the purges after the shah's return. But, this time, the shah seemed to be gone for good. The dominant feeling was that it was the end of an era. We feared the reaction of the fanatical monarchists who had remained silent up till then, or an about-turn from the royal army. Another coup d'état . . . Those were the catchphrases of the time. They told me to leave the city. "For my safety." But I wasn't in danger, for the Shah's regime had no more henchmen. It was too rotten on the inside to have them.

§

Regularly, depending on the events, the political climate, the police pressure, or the rumors that weren't always based in reality, I took refuge with Niloufar. Even the Doctor conceded that I was safer with them. During that time, he was still an influential man, and the police treated him with respect. Niloufar's mother welcomed me warmly, she was happy to contribute to the struggle in this way that would lead to the overthrow of her old enemy. As for Niloufar, she didn't seem at all affected by my presence, but I had learned to decipher the tiny signs of excitement that disturbed her usual indifference. She was like an unpredictable flower that would suddenly open, passing from one state to another in a matter of seconds. She would suddenly interrupt what had seemed to hold all her attention and invite me into her bedroom and lead me into the twists and turns of her reflections like a stubborn little girl, without a care for the time that passed. She was no longer the spoiled child that cared about nothing. She had become hypersensitive. Determined to face all the injustices of the world. She was walking in the footsteps of giants. Carrying the weight of the world. She wasn't afraid of anything. She wanted to respond to the call of the deep. Remain underwater until the final victory of the people. And she asked me to help her. She wanted me to transmit to her all that I knew in one sentence. In one word even, if possible. And at night, she would sometimes let me sleep in her bedroom. I am not very big, as you can see. At the time, I was much skinnier, and her couch suited me perfectly. I was happy. I shared her bedroom, breathed the air she breathed, listened to the melody of her breath, the crinkling of the sheets when she turned over. I woke up before dawn, I didn't have to move. From the couch, I let my eyes wander. The darkness of the room gradually dissipated, and I was able to see her. Sleeping in her bed, dressed in a simple shirt or in one of her legendary tank tops, her arms stretched along her body, her black jellyfish hair smeared over the pillow. I spent long minutes watching her closed eyes and the black arcs of her eyelashes. I ran over the sinuous paths of her body. She breathed slowly. Air filled her large free-diver's lungs. Her breasts undulated beneath the covers. The wrinkles of her forehead were erased, just like her dimples. I could have spent a lifetime staring at her. Carried out a bizarre relationship with her, just like the one Mohamad-Réza had lived during his nights, separated from her only by a window, sharing the night air and the song of the stars. Did he envision the same things as me? Or something more subtle, more exalting, more intoxicating? Didn't he possess the most beautiful part of her, despite everything? For the proximity she shared with me was not an advantage. If you knew her even a little bit, you knew that it was in fact the exact opposite. If I had slept in another room, I could have hoped. There would have been at least the tiny possibility that she would come in the middle of the night to upturn the established order once more, to which she alone held the secret. But here, in her bedroom, right next to me, she was putting the maximum amount of distance between us. Despite all my vain efforts, she turned me into the little boy that I was trying so hard not to be. She relegated me to the place of observer, hopeless lookout. No matter what I did, I was no better than Mohamad-Réza in her eyes, I couldn't even hope for more than him. To be considered as something other than a voyeur, a solitary pleasure-seeker, a masturbator. Objectively, I was even worse. Mohamad-Réza, at least, took the risk of scaling a wall, of putting himself in danger, naked. He hadn't promised honesty, fraternity, and camaraderie. He hadn't lied. He was true to himself. A desperate lover, devoured by an outsize desire. I was an impostor, aware and tired of my own schemes.

Despite what Niloufar's mother insinuated, her husband, that man we called the Doctor, didn't feel at all threatened by what was going on in the country. He had never dreamed of transferring his money abroad nor of leaving the country, as a number of his colleagues had done. He was even, in his own way, in solidarity with the people on the streets. Little by little, he started to speak nostalgically of his years in the Tudeh Party, his days of combat, his feats of battle. The revolt we were living in had made everything resurface in his mind, like the shipwrecked cadavers floating on the water. An ancient flame had reignited in his eyes. He, too, was secretly dreaming of his revolution. When I think about it, I am more and more convinced that at the end of the day there is never just one revolution, but a multitude of revolutions. Everyone makes his own. Everyone pursues his dream. Only, the sum of individual dreams does not amount to a common dream, but rather to a collective nightmare. So the Doctor, that old lion, was reliving his youth, remembering his meetings with his students, the unionists. He was recalling the relics of the speeches on the "fraternal" parties around the

Soviet countries. He had rediscovered the party's accent and somewhat outdated vocabulary. He was analyzing the causes of his failure, deploring those wasted years of combat that could have been avoided; he had forgotten nothing of those years. On those nights, after one of his tirades, blazed hot, he would take out a bottle of whiskey from his stash, serve us a double and start to dream, pretending not to notice his wife's mocking smile. We drank to the glory of the people. Those were good people. And they were the last. He spoke to me in a miraculous imitation of the accent of his fiercest enemy, his wife. It's true that, after the coup d'état in 1953, he had escaped by the skin of his teeth and had been able to slip by without passing through the checkout. But he would pay the bill years later, and with interest!

22 Bahman,[12] there was an uprising in Rasht, and everywhere else. Niloufar's mother had declared loud and clear that she wanted to "finish the job left undone thirty years ago." And for nothing in the world did she want to fail her mission, not this time. That day, the driver dropped us a few streets from the main town square. He wasn't able to go any further because of the traffic. We went the rest of the way on foot. Following on the heels of thousands of others. On the main square, in the middle of the crowd, the last king of Iran was solidly seated on his immense

bronze horse and had no intention of leaving. In one hand he held the reins of his pure-blooded steed, with its protruding veins and long mane, rearing, legs spread enough to see its imposing testicles and the immense penis in its sheath, no doubt implying the virile force of its rider, and, with the other hand, he was giving a military salute. He dominated the square, not at all worried about the rearing horse balanced on the platform, nor about the people swarming at his feet, growing louder and louder, more and more menacing. The general euphoria was at its height. The people were chanting aggressively: "Death to the king!" Their intentions were clear. They wanted to tear down the statue of the king. Everyone did the best they could. A dozen people had managed to climb onto the platform and were attempting to unbolt the statue. Others had slung a cord around the horse's neck and were pulling. The statue resisted. The horse was mounted on its hind legs, hooves solidly anchored in concrete, fixed in a final silent whinny, carrying on its bronze back what remained of its rider's waning power, the future fallen king. Niloufar's mother cleared a path in the crowd despite her weak shoulders. Putting her elegance and good manners aside, she successfully pushed the others away and advanced toward the statue. She was light and agile, as if the numbness of thirty years of sleep had suddenly left her.

She was almost running, forcing us to speed up to follow her. Once under the platform, she had found her youth again. She was crying out with the people, wanting to scale the concrete wall herself, down with the king and this time for good, even if it meant tearing down that nasty horse with her own hands. Breaking its legs with her own teeth. But, at the last moment, she opted to give her daughter a boost so she could climb in her place. She encouraged her to climb higher, and Niloufar climbed all the way up, finding herself on the horse's hind quarters in no time, then on the shoulders of the rider. She was the one who put the cord around the king's neck, as around the neck of someone condemned to death. An act that provoked immense joy in the crowd. And tears of joy in the eyes of a mother who was finally seeing her daughter achieve the work that she herself had begun thirty years prior. The crowd applauded and launched into frantic slogans, pulling on the cord to the cry of "Death to the king!" But the steed stood its ground, and its imperturbable master continued to salute the unleashed people. As if he were continuing to see his subjects, the same ones that had cheered in former days at the passing of the royal vehicle, chanting his name, rushing to kiss his feet. As if he were insisting on hearing that "Long live the king!" that those same mouths had so often uttered. "They reinforced it, the bastards," Niloufar's mother remarked with rage. She remembered that, under Mosaddegh, the horse had tilted more easily. Tilted, but not fallen! After the American coup d'état and the return of the Shah, they had erected it again so that it would continue to loom over the square, the cars that drove around, the to-and-fro of an amnesiac population. The same people that had cried "Long live Mosaddegh!" one morning and "Long live the king!" that same night. The same people who promised to take to the streets by the millions if someone tried to touch their liberty or their leader and who then hid the night of the coup d'état, when they had carried Mosaddegh away with his hands tied. Who had slept with their heads under their pillows so as not to hear the gunfire that split Fatemi's heart.[13] A people whose promises you should be wary of, for the masses are desperately shortsighted and endowed with a reptilian memory. The proof is that for two hundred years, at each major turn of history, they always make the worst choices. With each bifurcation, they travel down the worst path. Yes, the bronze beast had been reinstalled in 1953, and they had used that opportunity, predicting the days to come, to anchor it very solidly on its pedestal.

Then the cranes arrived as backup, with armed men who bluntly pushed people out of the way. They cleared everyone out by whipping their belts. The statue was ripped out in a cracking of concrete, a crumpling of iron, the din of motors pushed to full capacity and cries of "Allahu Akbar!" The iron horse fell, folded in two, its rider kissed the ground, the people stomped on it, spit on it, took photos of it, took photos with it, then took off under the beating rain, drunk with joy. The hangover would come later. Niloufar's mother was thrilled. She had had her revenge. The shah's reign was finally over. She was right, and the Doctor was wrong. The pitifully outstretched horse and the trampled king were the proof. The square emptied. We were able to resume the thread of the future, which could not under any circumstances resemble the past. Terrible mistake. We had forgotten the most important thing. Yes, the rider had fallen, but the pedestal was still in its place. And it wouldn't remain empty forever. Another statue would be erected there. Bigger, more ferocious, and more difficult to unbolt. A statue that didn't wear boots, but babouches, that didn't dress in a military uniform, but wore a mullah's cassock, that didn't salute the people, but God. Yes, my friend, we had erased "the shadow of God on earth" to put God in its place. Yes, God Himself.

Our small town had no statue of the king to tear down. Instead, we destroyed the movie theaters and vandalized drinking establishments, deemed symbols of the decadence of the former regime. When I saw the burnt carcasses of film reels thrown in the streets, our movie theater's seats ripped open, the smashed ticket booth and the torn posters, I should have asked myself questions. Asked myself who was capable of doing such a thing. What revolutionary explanation would I invent for those acts?

Our small town had two movie theaters. One that mostly played Persian films. That's how we learned about Iranian cinema. And the other, situated on a main avenue, showed foreign films: American Westerns, French dramas, Indian melodramas, and not long before the revolution, Italian soft pornos. The theaters were magical places, open doors onto the marvelous world that wrested us from the narrow and dusty streets of our daily lives, a world of adventures, beauty, and enchantment, a world that had to be somewhere at the end of the roads where those cars filled with strange passengers were driving. Thanks to the movie theater, those cars stopped, and their strange passengers got out in our city, walked into our lives: Fardin, Behrouz Vossoughi, Forouzan, Marilyn Monroe, Burt Lancaster, Amitabh Bachchan . . .

The cinema was important to the life of our city. With a few exceptions, even the most traditional families went out to the cinema. We went to the cinema Friday nights as a family and during the week with friends, skipping school. We went to the cinema to dream, see the world, take advantage of the dark theater to hold hands with a girl. So why was it destroyed? Why vandalize the drinking establishments? They said that the owners, as they tried to salvage their business, recognized their clients among the assailants. The same ones who came to have a drink after work. Even Mohamad-Réza's father, whose personal stash had enlivened our summer nights, had been at the head of a militia responsible for the destruction of several restaurants where alcohol was served. Why? Something was happening before our eyes, and we refused to see it. "It's a revolution," I explained to my disciples. "The future is now being built on the ruins of the past." I justified the unjustifiable. I told them that it was the inexorable revenge of the poor, the outcasts of the capitalist system, on the symbols of an unjust and unequal society. Bullshit. What poor? The most fervent Hezbollahis, like the father of Mohamad-Réza, were rich bazaar merchants. If it was revenge, it was that of the past on the future. That of the most reactionary religious archaism on a modernity that had been injected but not yet assimilated. The revenge of the peasants on the city-dwellers. And we, with our complicity, were only feeding the monster that was growing in the shadows, secretly multiplying. I didn't approve of the women protesting in Tehran and in the big cities, taking to the streets to protest having to wear the hijab. Worse still, I asked my female friends to wear a headscarf when they distributed pamphlets, so as not to offend the "religious sensibility" of the people. Yes, me. The Supreme Leader had taken the throne in Tehran. This time, the Shah would not return.

The disfigured offspring of the Islamic revolution was moaning in its basin, bathing in tears and blood.

A few days later, a large protest was organized in the city to support the new power growing in the shadows. It was the day before the referendum that would guarantee the rise of the Islamic Republic. A bogus referendum. Constructed around an absurd dichotomy: "Islamic Republic. Yes? No?" And no one took offense to that ridiculous question, which would trap us for decades. An immense crowd filled the city's streets. Who were these people? Where did they come from? We didn't know any of them.

§

Chamkhaleh was the spoils of war. A captive miscreant virgin promised to the vanquishers. The village was another symbol to destroy. It was taken without resistance. No one thought to defend its sandy paths, its beaches, its sea, and its morning sun. No one had thought to protect its strolling girls, its boats on the river, its summer flings. The summer arrived a few months later. Once more, the great exodus from the city toward the seaside didn't take place. It was, if I'm remembering correctly, a horrendously hot summer, but most people preferred to remain in town, even if it meant sweating like hell. The bridge was cut off to traffic and because of this the village had regained its former insular character. The difference was that this insularity was not to protect it, but to enclose it. Henceforth, you had to identify yourself at a checkpoint stationed on the bridge, as if to enter a military barracks. The armed Basij stopped the cars with an obvious hatred and rifled through them with an excess of inexhaustible zeal to destroy anything remotely related to fun and pleasure. Alcohol, obviously, but also music cassettes, whose magnetic strips were torn up yard by yard before the wide eyes of their owner, card games, backgammon or chess, annihilated with brazen joy, all was prohibited. As well as any material evidence of relationships between illicit couples or groups of men in the company of women. But the real misery for the vacationers began once past the checkpoint. There were mobile patrols that watched over everything. Flirting, laughing, games, anything that involved contact between the opposite sexes was strictly controlled. On the main road that led toward the sea, the shops were closed for the most part and within the rare few that were open, the owners displayed a funereal air. Worried like drug dealers on the alert. The macabre ambiance was completed by the speakers perched on the newly installed poles and that dissimulated verses from the Quran. Yes, the Quran, distorted by the speakers pushed to their limit, unintelligible. The antonym of Vaveli. As for Vaveli, it would become a public restroom. At the end of the main road, the sea was no longer in its place. We thought we were dreaming. The sea, the immense Caspian Sea, was no longer at the end of the beach. A wall of sand had been erected, high enough to obstruct the sight of the azure expanse. How was it possible? It was, of course, forbidden to scale the artificial hill to access the sea. One had to pass through an opaque portal, guarded by the Basij. But the real horror was on the other side of the wall of sand. Behind the entryway, the sea had been split in two. Enormous pillars had been erected in the water to support a dividing wall that extended far into the waves. In a signal tower, they separated the male swimmers from the female swimmers, the women on one side, the men on the other.

You understand . . . They had managed to transform the sea into a public hammam! A place for men to take a dip and a place for women to take a dip. And the worst part was the insane number of people. A new world of people. People who settled for the sea mutilated in this way. Summer vacationers like we had never seen before. Who were they? Where had they come from? These women who were bathing fully dressed, these men who were strolling in exclusively male groups. Unshaven, with extra-long bathing trunks.

I don't know if you can imagine the extent of the damage. The sea had become entertainment without pleasure. It was Chamkhaleh without its night strolls. Chamkhaleh without its bonfire, without its prowling boys, without its joyous swimmers. Chamkhaleh without its sea. A Chamkhaleh without Chamkhaleh.

That summer, Villa Rose experienced some timid activity. Stumbling painfully against the wall of sand, it resembled a besieged bunker. The German cousin had not come, nor the other friends, to brighten up the gloomy days. Niloufar went out rarely and no longer swam in the sea. She swam only once, and it was in the river, in a case of emergency. One night, she was strolling with her mother on the banks of the river where people had started going since they could no longer walk on the seashore. During their walk, they were alerted by screams. A boat had capsized, and several people had fallen into the water, including two children. The survivors, not knowing how to swim, clung to the skiff, but one child had still not resurfaced, hence the distressed cries of the parents. They say that Niloufar simply removed her shoes and then threw herself into the water. A few quick breaststrokes, as she was able to do, and she had reached the boat, but the child had already sunk. She immediately dove down to look. She remained underwater for a long time, so long that they thought she had drowned too. Then she reappeared, holding the vanished child in her arms. When she emerged from the water, she was of course completely soaked and her shirt clung to her body. They say that as soon as she was out of the river, she was stopped by the cold metal of a gun barrel pressed against her belly button, held by a young Basij who was probably asking himself if he had to pull the trigger or continue getting an eyeful. Niloufar had broken several laws: swimming in a forbidden place and exposing herself in an indecent fashion. The child was saved, but Niloufar, arrested by the mobile patrol, wasn't freed until several hours later and only after important family members intervened. Immediately after that incident, without awaiting the autumn rain, the inhabitants of

Villa Rose left Chamkhaleh and didn't return for several years.

During that time, I was very busy. My entourage grew every day. I traveled to different cities to host meetings. I was a good orator and packed the room every time. They treated me with respect. Niloufar followed my exploits. When she could, she would come listen to me debate. At the end of the night, we would walk together and continue the discussion on the way back. She would ask me questions, taking me by the arm, as she would have done with a brother if she'd had one. That's how it was for her, but not for the eyes that observed us in the street. We found ourselves again at Niloufar's house for our organization's internal meetings. Her mother welcomed us with hospitality. We had the illusion of being free, but it was rather due to the embryonic nature of the repressive machine of the new regime. Too good to last! One autumn day, a group of Islamist students attacked the United States Embassy and took its sixty-six American employees hostage. They were shown on the TV, hands tied and eyes blindfolded. The Islamists burned the star-spangled banner, then the Union Jack. An Iranian invention adopted by all the anti-Westerners. A few months later, Saddam Hussein publicly tore up the famous Algiers Agreement, considered humiliating, and unleashed his tanks on the oil-producing cities of Southern Iran. The Iran–Iraq War had been declared. The regime rid itself of the last men in suits still present within the ranks of power. Bani-Sadr, the first president of the Republic, was dismissed. The bloody attacks multiplied. A bomb exploded in the Islamic Republican Party headquarters, the only party in power. Seventy-five leading officials died on the spot. To make up for lost time, the repressive machine was doubling down. The Basij militia armed itself more and more. A ferocious repression began. The country plunged into its darkest years.

You know the rest. It's around this time that you were enlisted into the ranks of the dissidents. You must remember . . . As at the arrival of a storm, everything suddenly changed. Things that, a few days earlier, had still been permitted—walking with friends, buying books, traveling from city to city—were suddenly no longer allowed. At each entry into town, at each intersection even, the young armed militia controlled the traffic. Everyone knew instinctively that they had to obey. The war served as an excuse to muzzle society. Eroding the last scraps of freedom that had resisted the assault of the bearded men. Our town found itself twelve hundred miles from the front. So what were they looking for in the trunks of cars, in the bags of women, in the pockets of men? Weapons for the Iraqi enemy? There was a reason the Supreme Leader had described the war as a "blessing," a "gift from the heavens." Yes, that useless and deadly war served as grace and salvation for the Islamic regime. It gathered Iranians behind a new patriotic-Islamist ideology, with inconspicuous power. In the high schools, the classes emptied. The young people gathered in the mosques with budding beards, tied "*Ya Hossein*" bandannas around their heads, and then left for the front in jam-packed cars, shouting: "We are all your soldiers, Khomeini." You remember? To come back in small pitiful coffins, in a thousand pieces. That's how Ahmad, the most skilled bomb-maker, and Ali, the most daring Don Juan in Chamkhaleh, came back: between four planks of wood. We carried their coffins through the streets of the city and other young people left to take their place.

The death factory had started up and would run at full capacity for several years.

One day, we saw Mohamad-Réza leave. In front of the crowd assembled on the central square, he said goodbye to his mother who was crying beneath her brand-new black chador, bowed three times under the Quran his father was holding to bless him, climbed into the bus, and disappeared at the end of the road that turned at the foot of Leila Kooh.[14] Left without ever coming back, not on leave, nor in a coffin, disappearing simply and definitively from the life of our town. His absence was not really noticed. There had been so many others.

§

The terror operation was in full swing and kept rhythm with the tempo of the war. The new power was stripped of inhibitions, the first raids on dissidents' homes had already taken place. We had started to go into hiding. I returned to Niloufar's house for a bit. The rules of the game had changed, we had to behave differently. I didn't know if I could or wanted to play the game. The price to pay increased with each day. As you guessed, prison and corporal punishment were not my thing. And martyrdom even less so. I had to leave, go elsewhere, but where? The Doctor's house was no longer safe for me. The Doctor's past as a mayor, and his relationships with the fallen higher-ups, had caught up with him. He was unsuccessfully trying to keep his clients. His doctor's earnings were no longer sufficient to maintain the familial lifestyle. He suddenly realized that he had nothing. For all those years, he had set nothing aside, spending everything he earned without keeping track, on his friends, his sumptuous parties, and his mistresses. The town preacher had declared him impure during a Friday sermon and, ever since, his clientele diminished a bit more each day. Eaten away by the nostalgia of his unrestrained parties, his mistresses, and his games of backgammon, the Doctor was visibly growing thinner. And his alopecia only highlighted his thinness. He was sinking into a strange silence. Formerly so sure of his knowledge, so facetious, so verbose, he was now growing quieter and quieter, no longer taking part in discussions, letting his wife have the last word. He didn't like to play backgammon with me. Not because I played badly—I knew the rules and followed them all very carefully. The problem for him was that I didn't express enough joy when I won, or, worse, enough disappointment when I lost, and he didn't see the point in challenging an adversary whose self-esteem was so underdeveloped. So he invented an invisible partner to play games of backgammon that went on endlessly because, after each game, the winner or the loser would launch a new challenge, impossible not to accept. One could hear behind the door of his bedroom, sometimes until early in the morning, victorious laughs or disappointed cries, amidst the familiar noise of dice rolling over the shiny wood of the board.

The downsizing of the pomp of their lives was welcomed with a certain relief by Niloufar, but was more difficult for her mother. Since things had changed, she rarely left the house. Her friends, the benevolent Friday wives, had dispersed. Some had left the country with their families for the west coast of the United States of America, where the largest diaspora community of Iranians had formed. Others had switched sides, now went out veiled, in the company of a spouse metamorphosed into a bearded man. Her charitable works now served no purpose. At the house, Niloufar seemed even more distant than usual. She was busy with a strange task, leaving the house and returning at unusual hours. And when she was there, she often had a book in her hand, or was writing in a notebook, obscure notes in a tiny meticulous handwriting. A notebook with a laminated blue turquoise cover that I had given her for her birthday. The family was on the edge of imploding, in its last days. A thousand imperceptible details foretold it. One morning, they found Tamba dead. For a while, the little dog had been living practically forgotten in its corner. A recent memorandum had forbidden the ownership of pet dogs in Iran: they had been declared impure by the religious men in power. Deprived of its outings, after barking for a long time behind the door of the garden, the poor animal had finally abandoned the idea of going for walks and spent its days with its snout stuck out of a hole in the fence, content to observe the monotonous spectacle of the street. That's how we found him, lifeless, lying on the ground at his observation post. After Tamba's death, no more sporadic barking, no more pawing at the doors. The silence of the house had one less opportunity to be broken. The piano remained shut in the corner of the living room, the flowers wilted in the vases whose water was no longer changed, and the odor of oblivion spread through every corner of the beautiful house. And then I left the North for the capital. Tehran with its millions of inhabitants, its excess, and its anonymity seemed a better refuge for me.

Before leaving, I checked on Niloufar one last time. She had changed a lot, trading her appearance of a young insolent innocent girl for that of a woman. She still wore old shabby clothes, found here and there, but she exposed much less skin than before. No more extra-short skirt, no more extra-large tank top, no more extra-plunging neckline. Now she sported a bob hairstyle. The black jellyfish of the Caspian was now nothing but a legend. Those few years had also elongated her face, hollowed her dimples. But the most striking change was her silence. She no longer confided her intimate feelings in me and preferred to occupy her time with more "important" things. She was modifying her theses, posing theoretical questions, initiating debates that kept us going until late in the night. I let her do it. The spectacle of her moving mouth and the expressions of her face took precedence over what she was saying. I would agree with her wholeheartedly, then I would add a detail at the opportune moment, as I knew how to do so well, just so that her eyes would start to shine. Ah, those ideas that I sprinkled like live grenades that she filled her pockets with. Yes, I let her do it. Rather than warn her about the danger looming over her, I preferred to feel her admiring gaze on me and had no other goal than to prolong it infinitely. I reveled in her attention, I didn't neglect a single crumb of it, not an atom, and I asked for more still. Late, in her bedroom, drawing strength from the depths of my torments, I waited for her eyes to grow heavy, for sleep to take over her, and then I'd join her. Take her by the hand once more and bring her with me far away, to Chamkhaleh. Our Chamkhaleh. Cross the river by boat, travel beyond the wall of sand, jump the barbed wire, undress, and set off. Swim toward the open ocean. Go far, even farther than the fishing boats, the drifting nets, and the circle of seabirds, until all the noises of the world faded: the whining litany of the Quran diffused from the speakers perched on the roofs, the din of enraged men, the fury of the war, the cantor of "L'Homme nouveau," the class struggle in search of justice and equality, the parade of misfortunes. Listen to nothing but the sea, the sputtering of the water, the mysterious cadence of the depths. Walk with her on the hot sand. At night, in the dark mazes of alleyways and side roads, in the gleam of the stars, try once more to decipher their obscure geometry. Listen to the night. Its distant rumblings. But, in the silence, someone was singing in a beautiful voice tinged with a former love. He was singing love poems, those of Nazim Hikmet. That's the moment when I would withdraw my hand, the instant when everything became impossible again.

So I would plunge with her, searching for a bit of coral. I would follow her, and this time, I wouldn't stop myself, I would continue to descend without worrying about the lack of air, the tightness of my lungs. I would stay there. What did it matter . . . ? I would be one more shipwrecked person in that thousand-year-old sea.

I left Niloufar's house without saying goodbye to my hosts. The bus left at five in the morning from the main square. The same square where Niloufar's mother had been eager to topple the equestrian statue of the shah. At that hour, the city was already bustling. The construction workers were warming themselves around a fire burning in a hollow oil barrel. The cars were driving around the pedestal of the statue, still empty, now surrounded by green flags flapping in the wind. On the bus, I sat next to the window. A light freezing rain was falling. A couple crossed the wet crosswalk. The man was wearing a tight vest and wool pants, and the woman a loose-fitting dress and a headscarf with a colorful pattern on her head, clothes typical of peasants in the North. The man was hunched over and moving slowly, while the woman, vibrant and alert, was walking ahead, stopping regularly for him to catch up. I watched them for a long time. They were the only tangible truth in my field of vision. Nothing else was true, neither the imposing fresco of the Supreme Leader on the facade of the town hall, nor the tricolored flag with "Allah" in the middle formed by four blades, nor the veiled women, nor the war song filtering through the loud speakers. The couple had disappeared into the morning haze. The bus had finally filled. It set off arduously in a cloud of smoke, in the din of its tired engine, with the audacious promise of bringing us all the way to Tehran.

I set off leaving everything behind me, so many unfinished books like fleeting sandcastles abandoned by a child on the beach. The era had changed brutally. Our spring of freedom had turned into winter without passing through summer. Those few months of euphoria were coming to a close. Recess was over. No more public debates, no more free newspapers, no more sellers of dissident journals on the sidewalks. It was enough for the Supreme Leader to say that he didn't read a particular newspaper for the bearded assailants to destroy its headquarters. Bands of Basij paraded in the streets and attacked anyone who seemed against the religion, the revolution, anyone engaging in anything supposedly disapproved by the Supreme Leader. We had to go into hiding again. But the members of our committee, in our small town in the North, had been too exposed to disappear overnight. Even the most cunning, the most adept, would end up being caught.

Mahmoud "the jinn," who had earned his nickname because of his incredible agility, who was present at all the events, participated in all the debates, ate at all the banquets, was arrested on a bus coming back from a meeting with activists from a neighboring town. He would be tortured, then shot after six months of incarceration. He was twenty-eight years old. Behrouz, baptized "the calligraphist" because of his very nice handwriting in which he used to draw our movement's emblem on the walls of the city, was picked up one night in the street. He wasn't there to do graffiti, but to meet his girlfriend. They broke his fingers so he could no longer write, then they shot him after a year of imprisonment. He was twenty-five. Nasser "the tough guy," intransigent on political principles, was executed after a year and a half in prison, at nineteen years old. Then the others. One by one.

I learned later that they had all, without exception, been questioned about me, had all endured abuse aimed at finding out my location. Which was useless, because they didn't know. I was now swimming in the waters of Tehran.

I was picked up by Cyrus upon my arrival. We changed taxi three times. This journey alone seemed longer than going from one city to another in my region. Then we arrived at an apartment in the city center where we were welcomed by a young activist couple. I was introduced under a false name, Saïd, which was how I was known from then on in the organization. A basic introduction. I was a friend from the province. No point trying to hide it. My accent, typical of the North, was still strong. For the neighbors, I was invisible and, if someone showed up, they would introduce me as a friend of the husband, come to take care of a matter of inheritance. Life lived in secrecy came with strict rules. Our comings and goings were reduced to the bare minimum. The warning sign for the apartment was a flowerpot placed behind the window, visible from the street. If the pot wasn't in its place, we shouldn't enter, but go to the safe house, and if that too was compromised, that was that.

Cyrus left. I set my bag in a corner. Tehran vibrated behind the windows and I experienced my first night of insomnia, which was followed by many others.

I was accepted unanimously to the leadership of the party in the "central committee," as they pompously referred to it. The central committee, where decisions were made. The heart of the factory. The furnace of lies. I participated in secret meetings, organized in different locations in the city. It was a whole ritual. On the way, they made us close our eyes or lower our heads so as not to remember the address. When we were almost there, they made us enter the meeting place one by one. We carried various innocuous objects, a child seat, a watermelon, a bag of potatoes. In the house, there was no time to lose. Even if our organization wasn't armed, a military atmosphere reigned. We sat in a circle at the table, if there was one, otherwise on the ground. Everything was planned and timed. The agenda. The length of the speeches. The moderator. The meeting leader. In brief, it was a lot less fun than back in my town, where I had spoken and the others had listened. No place for discourse here. The rare times when I launched into one of my magisterial tirades, I was called back to order politely but firmly by my moderator comrade. No final applause, obviously. Then we left, preserving everything in our memories or in notes taken on cigarette paper. For the next meeting. We left the house as we had come, carrying our bric-a-brac in the other direction. We took our futile game very seriously.

§

During that time, I had countless nights of insomnia, as you must have experienced as well. That clandestine life is only fun briefly, then quickly becomes tiring. You spend the majority of your time trying to survive. You spend all of your energy hiding, respecting the rules of security, which in the end don't leave you any time for anything else, not to live, not even for the cause. Today, I am against all clandestine activity. If you believe in something, you should do it as much as possible, and if it's not possible, you shouldn't do it in hiding. You find another way. Secrecy doesn't serve any purpose. It's total nonsense. Even in countries under dictatorship. I would even say especially in countries under dictatorship. The dictator is afraid of the masses, not of individuals in hiding. You have to drown the dictator in the small freedoms that the masses allow themselves. A thousand tiny bites that the masses know to deliver to their enemy, once they've identified the enemy. But when the masses are not with you, as was the case in Iran at the beginning of the revolution, or in Nazi Germany, it's not even worth trying to resist. You simply have to hibernate. Let time do its work. That romantic idea of wanting to awaken the conscience through individual actions is as useless as writing "death to the wall" on the Great Wall of China. So we were busy breeding in a closed circle, feeding on our own worries, our own questions and certitudes. But the more the police pressure heightened, the more our existence became difficult and our mission impossible. The more we closed ourselves off in a parallel world, the more we distanced ourselves from the reality around us. The war swallowed its victims like a monster its daily pittance. The cities of Iran were falling one by one. Atrocious images invaded our daily lives. But we continued our debates. The death toll amounted to tens of thousands. The country was in crisis. We were still debating. We were revising our notes. We wanted to bring our socialist revolution to fruition. And when the world didn't correspond to our theories, it wasn't the theory that we blamed, but the world! It was the world that had a problem. And we had to find another theory as quickly as possible to explain the anomaly of reality. Quickly, find the counterattack. Quickly, get out the ideological forceps.

Around me, everything was false. Even to me, who was used to falsehood, imposture. Me, the fraud. I was out of my depth. The apartment, the objects that furnished it, the couple that lived in it, their first names, everything was false. Everything had been set up in haste, cardboard cutouts. It was a facade to make someone believe that there was a couple there, a family, a normal life. In vain. It would have taken less than a minute for someone to realize that these things weren't real. Even the pictures hung on the walls, meant to brighten up the apartment, were false. The sun setting behind the bare trees in the photo, the snowy summit in its frame, the couple embracing at the edge of the sea. What love? What sea? Love had been lost and the sea walled! In the official photograph of the wedding, we could tell the clothing was borrowed. The vest was too tight, the dress was too large, the smiles artificial. The rules of clandestine life stipulated that we communicate as little as possible to avoid knowing too much about each other. When it came to that rule, my hosts followed it to the point of abuse. They pushed the instructions to their paroxysm. Sleeping in separate bedrooms, they practically never spoke. They outdid each other in an attempt not to forget that they were the protagonists of a lie, that their marriage was nothing but a cover, clinging to false-hood out of fear that through lack of focus something real might happen. A gaze that lingered too long on the chest, a personal remark, a suggestive pleasantry. But, in time, reality would get the better of them. By hiding it, each instant exuded their repressed desire. Their suppressed embrace. And believe me, it was a sad sight to see.

It was over for me. My destiny was not written in any of the books piled in Niloufar's mother's wooden boxes, the books saturated with the smell of rice and hope for a better world. Destroyed, like an empty-handed gambler, I had nothing left to put on the table. The silence gnawed at me from the inside. I missed the North. I was living in Tehran, but that was just one more illusion, as if I were seeing the city on a TV screen, through thick glass. In truth, I had never gotten off the bus that had brought me here. The times when I went out alone, I got lost. I couldn't adapt to the dry air, to the dark and sterile blue of the sky, to the stench of the sewers, the packed sidewalks and the constant rush of people. I missed the rain. I missed the clouds. The verdant mountains, the river, the cascading rice fields, the salty wind, I missed all of it terribly.

I was afraid. I wasn't a complete idiot. I saw clearly that I was done for. Beyond the theory and the principles, it was enough to go from one end of Tehran to the other once to see that our cause was totally hopeless. Daily life had consumed the people. The war was affecting the country's economy. Everything was rationed. They were juggling the white market and the black market, where the prices shot up a thousand percent. They spent hours lining up for food staples. Survival took precedence over reflection and thought. A collective delirium, a general rage had taken over the country. People saw Khomeini's face in the moon. The mullahs went out with weapons over their shoulders. The Friday preachers delivered their sermons with guns in their hands. The most important matters were solved with reasoning that was summed up in a few categorical terms, spewed on a loop from the mouth of the already very old Supreme Leader. We wanted to defend the country against an enemy that we had invented ourselves. We were persisting in a revolution that was leading the country to chaos. In any case, my career was over. The path that should have led me to glory and fortune proved to be a dead end. Worse still, it turned out to be my Stations of the Cross. Yes, I was afraid. That was the reason for my insomnia. I already said it: I've never been courageous. Deep down, I knew that I was no heroic resistance fighter. I wasn't made for that destiny. Electric shock torture, cables whipped on the soles of the feet, nails ripped out, solitary confinement—no thank you. I was constantly on the alert. Footsteps on the staircase, a car stopped in front of the building, a slowing truck, voices on the sidewalk, everything scared me, they were going to arrest me. I was so afraid that I worried I would reveal my fear in my sleep, betraying it with a word, a cry, a gesture. I was living in a state of permanent alert. I was as wary of my friends as of my enemies. I imagined fleeing. But where would I go? Parand's father had sent me a letter with a considerable sum of money and a note reminding me that I could always count on him. That money was lying at the bottom of my bag. It was enough for me to go wherever I wanted. Even outside of the country, like you. But, at that time, no one dreamed of leaving the country. The wave of exiles abroad began a few years later. So another idea came to me. I pushed it away at first, but it came back with persistence. An idea so crazy that it makes me feel ill just admitting it. But I'll tell it to you. That's what I came here for, right? To tell you the truth, the whole truth. I was thinking very seriously and more and more often about turning myself in. Yes, simply giving myself up. Walking into a Pasdaran army base and confessing to them who I was. If I surrendered, it was likely I would receive special treatment. I would have the right to speak, I hoped. And if I could speak, I could manage, I was convinced of it. As I had done a few years earlier with the secret police of the former regime. After a few hours, the SAVAK agents ended up believing me. I hadn't received a single blow, not even a slap. I told you, I have the ability to be very convincing. I persuaded them that what I was doing was only subversive in appearance. I had proved that it was of more interest to them to let me go than to keep me in captivity. I could influence my peers, temper their ardor, keep them from veering into extremism. And they freed me. Better still, they had kept the matter quiet, leaving it to me to arrange how the information leaked.

There was no reason to think that what had worked so well with the Shah's secret police wouldn't work with the ignorant mullahs, the mechanics and butcher boys who had become impromptu inspectors and torturers. They had their weaknesses. You just had to find them. Their God, their faith, their obtuse observance of sharia law were all cracks through which I could meddle with their logic, infest it, and redirect it in my favor. I had read the Quran, *Nahj al-Balagha*, and other Shiite reference works. I could use them to my advantage. No, I wasn't worried. All I had to do was be myself. Abandon my position as a revolutionary leader. Take off the mask and present myself as I was. As naked, as weak as I was. I had to try. It was the best I could do. I would show them my real face—the face of a traitor.

The Doctor ended up giving in. He secretly delivered the baby of a woman sought by the police. His wife knocked on the door one night when he was alone in his bedroom, probably occupied by a game of backgammon with his imaginary partner. The Doctor opened the door. For the first time in twenty years his wife entered his bedroom, his wife whose existence he had stubbornly ignored. She stood opposite him, looked him in the eyes. Then she spoke to him in a conciliatory voice. It was the first time in far too long that she was finally speaking to him in that tone. Hardly had her hand slid over her husband's than he confessed that he loved his wife more than his games of backgammon, his friends, and all his mistresses combined. After listening to her, he packed up his medical bag and followed her.

He relapsed. When he was arrested at the bedside of one of his secret patients, and he was beaten and thrown in prison, his wife finally conceded grudgingly that the Doctor was perhaps not a bankrolled agent of American imperialism.

The war got bogged down in the swamps of Shalamcheh,[15] in the dust of deserted expanses in the south and the west of the country. The Tehran nights were broken up by the arrival of Russian missiles launched by the Iraqi army over the city. The Iranians retaliated with weapons supplied by Israel. Then the Iraqis dropped chemical bombs designed in the United States and made in Europe. The Iranians responded by crushing the town of Basra, within mortar range, and sending even more soldiers to the front. The operations came in quick succession with canonical names, Karbala 1, then Karbala 2 and 3. Karbala 4 was a total fiasco, unspeakable carnage. The Pasdaran had taken control of the war, annihilating the generals and the soldiers appointed by the former regime, who they replaced with autodidacts, whose apprenticeship in military strategy exacted a high price in human lives. Hundreds of young people died in order to seize a small town, a simple hill, that they would then cede to the next Iraqi counteroffensive. Despite the massacre, no one was interested in putting an end to the conflict. Not the mullahs, who had found in the war a guarantee of remaining in power. Nor the war leaders, aligned with the new businessmen who were earning dizzying sums by bypassing the American embargo. Nor the great European democracies, which were selling weapons to the warring nations, docile and solvent clients, because of their oil deposits. And not the Sunni Arab Emirati rich, terrorized by the ascent of an expansionist Shiite Islam. In brief, each group had its stake in the prolongation of the conflict. Macabre altars topped with the image of young martyrs had been erected in each corner of the street. The walls and doors were covered with photos of young soldiers fallen at the front. Always the same canonical three-quarter pose, the robot-portrait of the model martyr, budding beard, forced smile, eyes fixed on the camera, and that strange mystical breach outside the frame, the focus of the subject's stare as he contemplates death through us. The cemeteries expanded a bit more each day. Every family paid its tribute in fresh flesh. You remember, don't you? It was horrific.

§

And Niloufar was missing in action.

Her mother had reestablished relations with the Tudeh Party, which had been reformed after the fall of the shah. You've already heard the expression, I imagine: "Once a Tudehi, always a Tudehi."

The white-haired former leaders had returned to the country, and the party had reassembled its former members like an army of shadows. Why did those rumpled sixty-somethings, those established, important people and their children and grandchildren reunite to put the old rusty organization of the party back in motion? That question remained unanswered. And to do what? Exactly the same thing as under the shah, align behind the foreign politics of the Russian Big Brother! Watch out! At that time, the wall was still standing. They kept calling Russia the "country of Soviets." And the leaders of the Tudeh Party, still just as sly, still just as aligned with those in power, still just as foolish, had not understood even after forty years that you can't sleep with a bear without swallowing fur. They sent their base back to the slaughterhouse, but what was different this time, when things started to go off the rails, when the purges began again, even the kingpins let themselves be captured, preferring the jails of the Islamic government to the "golden" exile in the Soviet countries and its satellites. I don't know what Niloufar's mother's role was in the new Tudeh Party, nor the importance she held in the decision-making echelon, but she was arrested and spent five years in prison. They say that she was tortured savagely. So much so that when she was released, she was an old woman with white hair. Her legendary haughtiness was no more. She had a hunched back, and something was missing from her eyes: the insolent flame she had kept alive for all those years, fueled by the hatred of her husband, fed by her detestation of those who had succeeded in profiting off of social injustice, and through her denouncement of the capitalist system. Forgetting until her death that she had been a part of it.

Nilou was still missing. She was no longer there. After his release from prison, the Doctor had been banned from the medical profession, and his office had closed definitively. He was living as a recluse with one of his former mistresses. He was paying her expenses in exchange for a mattress and a few puffs of opium. Their beautiful house had been sold, with all the beautiful things it contained. Niloufar's mother, taking refuge with her brother, died there a few months later. Upon her death, they found in her pocket a crumpled photograph of her next to the Doctor, squeezing Niloufar with her braids, her chubby little girl legs and her white dress, on the terrace of Villa Rose in Chamkhaleh.

But where was Niloufar? I should have suspected. Everything suggested that she would disappear: her silence during the last few visits, her change in attitude, her somber habits, her strange questions. If I had been a bit less preoccupied by the reflection of my own image in her eyes, a bit less plunged into the hollow of her dimples, less absorbed by the lines of her neck, if I had listened to her words instead of staring at her mouth, I would have understood that she was hiding something from me, that she was working on a secret task, an obscure enterprise. But I was near her for something else. With her, I had never emerged from that pale blue that attracted me to the bottom of the sea. To the silence of the waters. While she, to the contrary, had listened to me. Had believed me, alas. Just like me, she was seeking her revenge on life, the terrible revenge of a spoiled child who wants to pay all at once for all the favors she had received despite herself. Pay for the life that all the world envied. Pay for her father's car and the driver who dropped her off each morning at school. Pay for the house that was too big and too beautiful. Pay for those rich, refined meals she had savored. For her father's arrogance. Her mother's elegance. For poor Parand, who she had ignored and who had died as a martyr. For that unlucky stammerer Mohamad-Réza, who had been humiliated in front of her. She wanted to pay for all of it. In one go, with damages and interest. So she had joined the most radical extreme left movement, who were also the most narrow-minded, proponents of armed struggle and urban guerrilla warfare. An ideological movement imported as contraband from Latin America, during the time of the shah. The "Ashraf Movement."[16] Suicidal purists. I told myself that she could be in the mountains of Iranian Kurdistan, a Kalashnikov in her hand.

§

Forgiveness does not exist. Even if you give me your absolution, I will not be delivered. My faults will not be expiated. I know that. I will have to pay. That's how it goes. That's justice. I admit it. I have always decided my own actions. I remember when, as a child, I discovered in myself a firm resistance to guilt. People need to confide in someone. Not me. As a child, when I was caught after doing something wrong, I never confessed. Even when I was caught red-handed. I continued to deny, or remained stoic. I never pleaded guilty. Never asked for forgiveness. What worried my mother wasn't the lack of a confession, it was that I never claimed my innocence, even when I was accused for no reason. All I did was enclose myself in an impenetrable silence, while continuing to stare my accusers straight in the eyes. I know that at every moment, at each turn in my life, I always chose the shortest path toward the fulfillment of my desires. I never encumbered myself with good and bad. I was indifferent. It was part of my nature.

A gift or a celestial curse? I don't know. And so I would walk around Tehran for hours without looking at anything other than my feet. The streets continued on infinitely. I didn't need to lift my head. The landscape was changing around me, the density of the population, the background noise, the accents of merchants on shop steps, voices of women chatting in front of their doors. I found myself in working-class neighborhoods, in the downcast areas in the south of the city. If there was one advantage to Tehran, that was it. Its crooked and borderless geography. The labyrinth of the streets, rarely uncorking onto a dead end. The moans of the muezzins floating in the air, suspended like fog on the branches of burnt trees, on the electricity lines and on the windowsills. I was walking, and I couldn't stop myself. I crossed and crossed again, over the dry gutters that cracked the macadam, between the slabs of concrete, those overturned mirrors of the city. I shouldn't have been there. I was too visible. In that time, you could be arrested for less than that. But I didn't want to acknowledge that. Those days, I was, I know now, in full gestation. Yes, gestation. My body was secreting a new substance. My soul was exhaling the breath held from a free-dive in my past. I felt something that I would know how to identify only later, much later: the soft and smooth blade of guilt working its way through my entrails, patiently cutting me to shreds.

Niloufar left one day, saying she was going to visit a friend in a neighboring city. She had taken a bag and a few pieces of clothing and had not come back. She had made just three phone calls, not one more, to say that she was well and that we shouldn't worry about her. That she would be back soon. This was something she had done count-less times. But I knew that she wouldn't come back that time, and that it was because of me. I had sent her to the slaughterhouse with my ideas, my guilt-inducing speeches. By working on her patiently, molding her, for years. I had done it, I know, I knew. Then I had abandoned her, alone, in that violent world. A world that I had contributed to safeguarding instead of fighting. I had contributed more than a stone to its structure, I had defended its principles and sung its praises. I might not have been mounted on the platform, but I had given wretched preachers a leg up. I had certainly not lit the fire, but I had held the torch. I had not killed, but I had dug the graves. Without regret. I've told you already; I felt no regret.

So why did walking aimlessly in the streets of Tehran engender in me the desire to go back down the thread of history? I wanted to redo my life, go back to the very begin-ning. Don't ask me why, but something in me was saying that I could make it so that the bullets shot back out of bodies, the shrapnel from the earth, so that the overturned fields would regain their serenity, so that the wall would never have been erected in front of the Caspian, so that the fire would still be burning on the beach during those short summer nights, surrounded by Hamed, Parand,

Mahmoud, Parviz, and Behrouz. Mohamad-Réza would still be singing the poems by Nazim Hikmet, with a flame in his eyes.

Every day, I pushed back the deadline to hand myself over to the Pasdaran. And the time that was passing made the story I wanted to tell them all the more difficult to swallow. The fear of being arrested knotted up my insides even during the day. I almost never went out anymore. Every time I went to a secret meeting, I told myself that it would be the last. But I was there at the next one. Everything continued until the raid. Until one of the group members, captured by the secret services, sent the entire organization into flight.

One day, coming back from a committee meeting, I saw the small flowerpot was no longer in the window. I followed the procedure. As planned, I passed the payphone situated on the north side of Vanak Square several times, but no one came to get me. I was in the street, left to my own devices. Not far away, on Molla Sadra Street, I slowly walked in front of the Pasdaran station without stopping. It was too late to hand myself over. Even with my prodigious talent for persuasion, even by recounting the cleverest story in the world, I wouldn't have been able to get myself out of this. Not this time. It was over. I had lost all credibility. Turning myself in would have looked like an act of desperation. The hideouts were falling like dead leaves. The Pasdaran army was kicking down doors and scooping up members of the organization. Someone had beaten me to the punch and agreed to tell them everything. Tehran had transformed into a hunting ground, and I was the prey. I spent my first day in taxis and buses that hauled me north to south, east to west, like a lost package. I felt like I was being watched, followed. Fear had put me on edge. Everything frightened me: the passersby, their stares, the cars that drove near me, the people who walked behind me. Then the sun set at the other end of the city, the night came, my first night of wandering.

I couldn't stay with any acquaintance living in Tehran. In those chaotic times, even the legendary familial hospitality no longer existed. The hotels and guesthouses had to be avoided. Then I had an idea. I bought a suitcase, stuffed it with cheap clothing and, that night, I went to the train station, at the end of what used to be Pahlavi Street, renamed Valiasr Street, where I bought a ticket for the farthest destination I could find. In the early morning, I was in Mashhad, more than six hundred miles from Tehran. I didn't leave the station; I made the trip back in the other direction. Then I started again the next night and continued for several nights. That's how I started my strange pilgrimages to the four corners of the country, with Tehran as my epicenter. Like the books of the Tudeh Party, in their bags of rice. A contradictory convoy, sent back endlessly. I saw quite a bit of the country. The arid plains, the mountains, the snowy summits, the verdant valleys, the furious torrents, and the seas of sand. I traveled through it, the villages, and even cities that aren't on the map. I found myself in nasty hostels, where I sometimes slept on the ground, among exhausted travelers, worn out and stinking. Over time, I would start to resemble them. I didn't recognize myself anymore. I had their moronic air, I was dirty. I think I was in each of the big cities of the country at least once, with the exception of the Southeast because of the war, and the North to avoid being recognized.

When the train or bus arrived, I would wander around the station, without ever venturing into the city. All those stations looked the same. Surrounded by cheap dormitories, short-term hotels, packed and cheap restaurants. For some time, another element added to this landscape: war icons. Every available surface was occupied by effigies of martyrs, amateur frescoes depicting war scenes. Sometimes, when I had a bit of time to kill, I would bathe in a public bath.

It was my favorite thing. I would doze off in the heat of the hammam, I would abandon myself to the hands of the professional washer, I would put on clean clothes and take the train or the bus in the other direction.

As a native of a region isolated by the Alborz Mountains and the Caspian Sea, I had no idea of the country. I discovered it from behind my window. I spoke to strangers, I shared their meals, their worries, their worlds. I was far from books, from polished speeches, from lies. I was living in the real world. I could have continued that way for a long while—in my bag, I had enough money to last me years. But one night, getting off of the bus, I found myself in my hometown. How? I never really knew. I only remember the trip. Leaving Tehran, then the Qazvin plains, flat and dry, then the climb up to the Harâz mountain pass, then the olive trees of Manjil and the gusts of wind, the long tunnel beneath the Alborz Mountains and the drizzle of Guilan that started to fall on the other side. That's when the windshield wipers started up and stayed on for the remainder of the journey.

I arrived at night, as always. The town was in a peaceful slumber, nestled around its bazaar and its double-arched bridge, folded in on itself under the rain. I walked without thinking. Without lifting my head. I could have found my

way just by following the noises, the smells. A few rare passersby walked by me without a glance. After ten minutes
of walking, I crossed the bridge. It was the rainy season,
and the river was flooded. The dark, torrential water was
wrapping, menacingly, around the pillars. Then I detected
a scent of rosewater and camphor. I was in front of the
mosque. I had arrived. In the small cul-de-sac, I stopped
in front of the metallic double-leaf door. It was three in
the morning. The door of our house awaited me with the
incredulous eyes of its two iron knockers. Those concentric
circles had always coldly spied on me. I had returned to the
ground zero of my destiny. Not as a conqueror, but in the
skin of a vagabond. There was nothing for me here. It was
no longer my house, and the people who lived there were
no longer my parents. I had made a mistake. I shouldn't
have been there. I turned around. I had to flee. No matter
where. Then the door opened, and I saw the face of an old
woman who strangely resembled my mother. Behind her
was my father, hair white, back stooped.

The table was set, my favorite meal awaited me, stuffed
eggplants with crushed walnuts. I sat down, I started to eat,
the old couple stared at me in silence. I fell asleep almost
as soon as I lay down in my bed. I was home.

Once more, I had to remain invisible, but this secrecy was more bearable to me than my previous life. I suddenly had time to reflect, to read. Of course, all my books had disappeared. My parents had gotten rid of them. A rather common occurrence in those years. Books were thrown out by the dozens, by the thousands, buried, burned, flung into the water. Concerned families set about the task quickly, deeming the books harmful for whatever reason, their title, their cover, the name of the author. I dug around the family library, among the few books that had been spared by the parental censure. There was, of course, the indispensable *Divan* of Hafez, the Quran, the *Nahj al-Balagha*, but also my father's books, the ones he kept in his own personal cabinet, where, as a child, I had found with stupefaction the almost naked photo of the voluptuous singer Hayedeh. I read *Amsal o Hekam* by Dehkhoda, *Masnavi* by Rumi, *Rubaiyat* by Khayyam, then more obscure books, like *Kitab al-Kafi*. Then I reread them and reread them again. With each reading, they seemed different. They were saying the same thing. But I was changing. I was growing older as I turned the pages.

My parents asked me no questions about my years away from them and the reasons for my return. I was there, and that was enough for them. I lived by the schedule of the house. My father got up at six in the morning. He rushed through the rapid couplets of his morning prayer, uttered without conviction, his voice muffled by the whirring of the samovar sputtering in the kitchen. Once dressed, he had his breakfast, a few mouthfuls of bread and cheese dipped in sugary tea, put on his shoes with the help of an old shoehorn, then left the house. He went to work on foot. No longer a silkworm merchant, just a tailor, without any surplus clients, he no longer needed his moped, which he had sold anyway. As soon as the door shut behind him, my mother turned off the samovar.

She woke up long before my father. She spent some time first in a dark room, praying. Her relations with God were essentially confidential, like an affair. She granted herself the right to interpret the rules and religious rites as she pleased. She took liberties with the divine. For example, I knew that she replaced the monotone chant of Al-Fatiha and the piercing Ayat al-Kursi of the five prayers with other verses from the Quran, which she chose depending on her mood in the moment. Then she sang the entire day. Since my earliest memories, she had always sung, but now, for the first time, I had the time to really listen: it was a sort of improvised blues. She was complaining about her life, her destiny.

Often, at night, I would sit in front of a window that overlooked the street. I would listen to the familiar murmur of the river flowing a few steps away, the rain falling on the roofs, the water gurgling in the gutters as before. But something had changed, which I noticed without ever going out. That city was no longer the city I had left behind me five years earlier. It was dying in silence. It seemed deserted, in mourning. I could no longer hear the racket of children when classes ended, the ruckus of young people at night, the songs of drunks in the middle of the night . . . The only thing that remained was the slinking gait of opium addicts at dawn, coming back from the dens.

One night, a car honked in the street, three unambiguous beeps, which suddenly wrested me from my torpor. But no one had had wind of my return. And besides, all my former friends had disappeared, taken by the war or imprisoned, some shot, others on the run. Hossein was waiting for me in front of the house, like in the good old days, at the wheel of his busted car. Hossein was probably the last of my friends from my high school days who was still around. He had always been indifferent to my renown, to my status as a political activist, to the solemnity I displayed in public. Even when I had reached the height of my glory, he would still tap me on the shoulder, like when we were in school, to heckle and tease me. He had the ability to bring out the dreamer, the shy boy I was at heart. With him, I could finally let my guard down, take off the mask and exist without shame. He probably owed his survival to his political indifference. Even at the most decisive moments of the revolution, he didn't get involved. He had followed all the uproar with a touch of condescension, as if it didn't concern him. A good truck driver's son, he dreamed of only one thing: becoming a truck driver in his turn and establishing a connection between our town and Tehran. A dream that he would realize a few years later.

I never knew how he had learned of my return. In any event, I climbed into his car, and we took the road bordered with marshes that led to Chamkhaleh. I had nothing to fear. The village was completely deserted. The cold and rain had chased everyone away, including the Basij. Hossein drove me to a cottage I had never been to before. Clearly, he had planned it out. The small house was heated. There were things to eat and drink. As soon as we sat down, he lit a brazier mischievously, to heat up an opium pipe. I had never tried opium, but I knew it would be pointless to resist.

It was winter. The Siberian winds shook the windows and blew through the zinc slats. Hossein seemed to know what he was doing. He must have had practice to be able to handle the pipe with such dexterity, bring it to the right temperature, then, after cutting the opium, place the piece in the right spot, heat it up so that the perfumed and velvety smoke would rise just enough, find its way through the hole in the pipe and arrive at its destination. After a few puffs, I felt a knot unravel in my chest, my muscles relax one by one. I don't know if you've ever tried it? In the moment, in any case, I finally understood why people abandon everything for this feeling of comfort, whose extent I had barely glimpsed. Already, by the second puff, I felt that I was breathing more easily, as if air was penetrating my lungs without encountering any resistance. The world had become small, so small that I could take it in my hand and put it in my pocket. Its troubles, its vicissitudes, its disasters were far away, they seemed futile and insignificant. We left the house, high as kites, for a short walk. Between fits of laughter, we embraced each other and made promises as sincere as they were untenable. But, mostly, we scratched each other. Yes, we spent the majority of our time scratching each other. Opium makes the skin ultra-sensitive, as if each cell of your skin were suddenly endowed with an autonomous intelligence. We scratched each other slowly and mutually, in a kind of virile and fraternal caress, floating in our narcotic euphoria.

As if we had been attracted by a lover, our steps in the deserted streets led us toward Villa Rose. It was standing there, sad and silent, like a washed-up cruise ship. Beneath the silver light of the moon, it seemed smaller and drabber than before. The bad weather had faded the pink color of its facade, turning it into a pale yellow. The sea had advanced and was unfurling at the foot of the black gate, now rusted, and its outer wall, which we skirted. I climbed on the electric pole behind the building to step over the wall and jumped into the backyard. Hossein stayed in the alley to keep watch. The doors and windows of the villa had been sealed. The terrace, covered in seaweed and dead leaves, testified to several years of abandon. I made a tour of the house. Nothing remained of its splendorous years, of its erotic aura engendered by the beautiful occupants of times past, of its powerful magnetism. I retraced my steps. Just as I was about to hop back over the wall, something caught my eye. The window of the garden shed, broken for a long time, had been replaced with plastic, and bits of fabric and cardboard acted as a door. As I approached, I got the feeling that someone was in there. Niloufar?

§

I'm telling you, despite the years, I remember the shiver I felt in that moment. My blood completely froze in my veins, and the euphoria of the opium dissipated all at once. I pushed on the old unhinged door and entered. There was an old blanket, rolled up in a corner, melted candles, piles of newspapers. And, on the windowsill, three seashells in a row. Why did that make me think of Niloufar? Why was I so sure she had been hiding there? I had no proof; it was just a hunch. But who else could have been hiding there? What hand other than hers could have placed those seashells on the windowsill? I had missed my meeting with her, the last one. That's what I thought then. I was wrong, of course—there would be others.

Niloufar had not gone into exile in the mountains of Kurdistan, as I had imagined. She had returned to Villa Rose. That's when my mother told me that she had come to see me. She had even stayed with my parents for a few days. My mother had stuffed her with her finest dishes because she had seemed so emaciated, weak, sick. She had slept in my bed. Then she had taken off again, without leaving a message for me. Where had she gone? Perhaps she was still in the area, with a member of her father's family I didn't know about. I could search for her. I would have confessed everything to her, as I am to you today. Even if I would have come off as a traitor, a terrible person, even if she would have hated me, I would have told her that I had lied. Maybe I could have broken her deadly certitudes, her dangerous faith, by breaking myself, the deceptive icon that I was. Tell her that I had never believed those words, those ideas, that it was all lies, an affect, a pretext to exist in the eyes of others, hers first and foremost. Then she might have changed her mind. Would it have saved her? Perhaps. But I did nothing. I didn't try to find her.

I had to get back on the road soon. No matter how high, no matter how thick, the walls will always reveal what they hide. Even drawn in front of the windows, the curtains leave a glimpse of the shadow that stands behind them. My presence at my parents' house couldn't remain a secret forever. So I packed my things. I put my money at the bottom of a bag, under a few articles of clothing, and threw the love poems of Nazim Hikmet on top, the only book I never got rid of. Then I boarded the bus for Tehran. As usual, I left at nightfall. A powerful sadness weighed on me. It didn't dissipate until after the long Manjil Tunnel.

The night before my departure, I sensed a presence in my bedroom. It was my father. I wasn't surprised. When I was a child, he often came in like that, discreetly, late at night, on the way back from his silkworm farms or his workshop. He would approach my bed on tiptoe. I would pretend to be sound asleep. Did he realize? I never knew. He would lean over and stare at me for a moment. Then he would stroke my forehead with his hand, rough like sandpaper, before placing a kiss on my cheek or my forehead. Those might have been the only caresses I ever received from him. That night, his kiss was firmer, lingered longer than in the past. I think it was the most affectionate kiss he'd ever given me.

The Guardians of the Revolution picked me up at the bus station; I'd barely even set foot in Tehran. Four bearded men in khaki uniforms. I gave them my hands almost with relief and, on the seat of the huge Toyota that drove me to Evin Prison, I abandoned myself to the contemplation of the city through the window.

Imprisoned in a country at war, as an enemy of the state: you could say that I'd hit the jackpot. What could I expect from my frightened and feverish jailers, uncertain of their own futures? In those years, life wasn't worth much. Hundreds, thousands of soldiers gave theirs each day on the battlefield. Death fell from the sky, walked in the street. We breathed it in like air. So what value could the life of an opponent have, who on top of it is an infidel, a communist? Even just those few syllables that made up *"komonist"* sounded like a sentence.

And yet I survived. After a few days of torture, they brought me to a dark room, warm and humid, like a Turkish bath. I cleared a path in the darkness, between the bodies that shared the poorly defined space, to the back wall. I had to wait for the light of day to grasp the incredible number of prisoners there. You, too, must have had that experience. I'll spare you the details. If someone had told me that I would live three years in that hole, I wouldn't have believed them. Even three days inside there seemed unbearable to me. Each night, in the wet heat of bodies, eyes riveted to the small opening at the top of the wall, I was certain that most of us wouldn't leave that place alive. Fear was always in our eyes, all the more so because we were young, for the most part. Some of them even looked like children. They would cry at night because they missed their parents' houses. Others had lost their minds and filled the cell, day and night, with their screaming and nightmares.

Almost every day, they fetched a handful of men. Many never came back, or if they did, they were in a very bad state, beaten, broken. Sometimes they forced us to watch these scenes of public repentance, during which the leaders of dissident parties confessed to implausible crimes. I awaited my turn. But something told me that I would get out. I knew my jailers better than anyone. Thanks to my mother, daughter of a mullah, and thanks to my father's books, I knew their thoughts, the rules they were abiding, their weaknesses. I preferred to deal with the old Hezbollahis, the educated Hajji, rather than the young idiots. With the former, I could at least stagger through the twists and turns of religious thought. My knowledge of the Quran and the *Nahj al-Balagha* had an impressive effect on them. I also knew how to gain the confidence of my jailers, my torturers, by commending their devotion and the difficulty of their task. They slowly warmed to me. That's how I survived the interrogations, the humiliations, the heavy-gauge electric cable whipping on the soles of my feet. I evaded the traps; I slipped through the net. I told you, I am a survivor. It's written in my DNA. Evin Prison was *The Raft of the Medusa* and my talents as a man-eater would come in handy one more time. Yes, like you, like everyone there, recounting their story, I ate the slimy and bitter flesh of friends, comrades, and brothers.

At night, I drowned myself in the pale and infinite blue of the Caspian. I had become skilled at holding my breath. I could leave the reality of this world to the others, abandon myself to the call of the deep and slowly sink. Thus, sitting amidst my comrades, more than six hundred miles from the Caspian, enclosed between four walls, I was able to indulge in the pleasure of asphyxiation, the approach of death, in my head. Each night I descended a bit deeper, each time I went a bit further. Down there, in the shadows, I searched for Nilou. I watched for her soaked, silken hair, undulating over her shoulders, the shimmering sparks on her long legs, on her powerful arms, the sparkle of her almond eyes. She was waiting for me.

The cell emptied and filled according to an obscure logic. The new arrivals took the place of those who left, who were transferred or liberated, but mostly executed. There were the passing birds, those who would be hoisted on the gallows or pumped full of lead in no time, and the "long-term" visitors, those who, like me, remained, settled into their corners, started businesses. I had a designated place in a corner of the cell, with the privilege due to my years served.

Little by little, the population of our jail stabilized, after the tidal waves of the early days. By listening to the conversations of the prison employees, I had surmised that the war was about to end. Our liberation was near, we thought. But that was far from true. We were deluding ourselves. The worst was yet to come.

§

The summer of '88 arrived like a bad promise, and the Supreme Leader issued his grand fatwa, which he wanted to see executed before his death. They were to empty the prisons of all the dissidents, starting with the Mojahedin of the People. The war had ended without the Pasdaran needing to attack Baghdad on their way to Jerusalem. They had to get rid of the bitter taste of the Iraq peace treaty, which the Supreme Leader himself had called "a cup of poison." What was the antidote? Who would pay the high price for our defeat? We would, the already-captured enemies. The troops without a flag, without a leader, and without weapons, who represented the forces of evil. You remember, don't you? During the three months of summer '88, thousands of prisoners, even those who had already been judged and were finishing their time, were sentenced again in summary trials and for the most part sent to the gallows, by a commando unit formed of three mullah judges. The silent massacre of five thousand defenseless men and women. And once more, I survived. I would stay long enough to learn the true suffering of the survivor. The infinite pain of the immortal. In spring '89, the prison was almost empty. We could now breathe the oxygen shares of those absent from the air of the cell. Spread our legs in the space that was no longer occupied by those who had left. It was our own paradise. Death was no longer lurking, and, like all the captives of the world, we could finally die of boredom.

Then, one morning, they came to get me while I was sleeping, with a feverishness, a nervousness that presaged nothing good, like in the early days of my incarceration. It happened sometimes, when a comrade was grabbed and interrogated, revealing a few names, casting an unexpected spotlight on a corner of shadow, where another person like me was holed up quietly. So we were back to the good old methods, the slaps and insults, the cable blows on the soles of our feet. It usually didn't go further than that. A few rough hours, nothing more. But, this time, things felt more serious. The guards didn't leave me the time to get dressed and, after handing me a hood, they led me across a good part of the prison, which was unusual. What was happening? Had a large fish fallen into the net? Most likely, but who? For a long time, there hadn't been any large fish swimming in the troubled waters of the country. They were dead, incarcerated, or in exile. They sat me on a metallic chair, in the middle of an empty room, where they left me for a few long minutes. Then I heard scraps of conversation, and soon the sound of footsteps in the hallway. The door opened. Several people entered the room. Instinctively, I readied myself for the blows.

Instead, I heard another pair of footsteps, more discreet, more muted, a friction of plastic sandals on the floor. I knew that sound well. The footsteps of a prisoner. They stopped near me. "Take off your hood" they ordered me. I obeyed. Almost as soon as I had revealed my face, they commanded me to hide it again. "You know him?" asked a voice. The question was directed at another prisoner. A barely audible "yes" was spoken. "Louder!" bellowed the same voice. There was a moment of silence, heavy, unending, after which I heard a resounding "Yes!" Strong, resolute, cutting. It was the voice of a woman. Of Niloufar.

Perhaps you have had similar experiences? It's in those moments that you realize everything you've done in your life had no other purpose than to lead you to that exact moment, that exact place. Each day of your life was drawing you nearer to it, preparing you for it. In a certain way, even your birth predestined you for it. And voilà, there you are!

That's when I saw, from beneath my flour sack whose thick fabric was permeated with the scent of all those who had worn it before me, a mix of sweat and the odors of scalp and dried blood, that's when I saw the feet of the prisoner who was standing before me. And that sight froze me with fear. In the thick black socks, in the compulsory bottle-green sandals, I glimpsed swollen ankles and deformed shins. But where were the slender legs, the thin joints, of Niloufar?

"You know him then?" the man asked again. "Yes," the voice repeated, tired. "And how do you know him?" insisted the interrogator. "How do I know him?" repeated the prisoner with an arrogance that was absolutely Niloufar's. A few seconds passed, before she added in a tone full of disdain: "He's my cousin." And, without her saying it, I heard the implied "dickhead" addressed to the man.

The wet smack of a hand slapping a face made me jump. Then other blows followed, sounds of footsteps, creaking of chairs, shouts. Niloufar seemed not to want to let it happen and yelled insults without worrying about the consequences.

When it was calm again, someone asked me to stand up and face the wall, before tearing off the hood. The light made me close my eyes for a few moments. Then I opened them again and turned around. I wanted to see Niloufar, I wanted to see my work, the fruit of my machinations. She was mine once again. My God, what had they done to her? She had a devastated face, hollowed by fatigue, her skin wrung dry and her gaze empty. Our eyes met and remained fixed on each other's for an amount of time I wouldn't be able to describe—a second, a minute, an eternity. Then, on her impassive face, which displayed neither fear, nor hatred, nor anything, an expression appeared, like a smile, that uncoiled over her blue lips. It was almost a laugh, her former laugh, intact. She was still the "Nilou" of my memories. I couldn't wrest my eyes from her, deaf to the cries addressed to me, to the blows that were now raining down on me. Perhaps I was seeing her for the last time. Then I saw her lower her eyes. My cheeks were burning. How many times had I been slapped? I didn't know. But I felt nothing. I lowered my head, too. In the silence, I could make out her breath, the same breath she had when she resurfaced from a long dive, triumphant, a seashell in her hand.

There was a commotion around us. People were coming and going constantly in the room, which was packed. And yet the count was not complete. They were waiting for someone. He was on the way, he would arrive in just a moment. I tried for a few seconds to forget that Niloufar was at my side, to gather my spirits. Clearly, she had not yet confessed anything. The freshness of her wounds, the vigor with which she had rebelled just now, reinforced my hypothesis. She was hiding something from them, but what? A name? An address? They wanted to make her talk through any means necessary. They were searching for her weak points, a crack in the wall that she had put up around herself. And that crack was me. At least, that's what they thought. If not, what was I doing there?

As I would learn later, Niloufar had been arrested in the house of a sympathizer. She had hidden there, even though she knew that the house was no longer a secure hiding place. But she hadn't had a choice. She was sick, eroded by a fever, prone to bleeding. They had found her in the bed, soaked with sweat and blood. Despite her state, she had managed to throw herself out of the car driving her to prison. She had run along several streets, crossed several blocks of houses, and, in the end, had jumped a wall, nearly succeeding in shaking off the militias, but was denounced by a Hezbollahi who had seen her pass. And so Niloufar was nabbed in a dead end, exhausted, betrayed by her sick body and by a man who was, by a stroke of bad luck, on the wrong side.

The background noise suddenly changed. Everything became quieter, as if someone had lowered the volume of the room. Even Niloufar had awoken from her semi-consciousness. I hadn't been mistaken. Someone arrived, a guest of high rank, even, judging by the length of bows addressed to him. I heard a name repeated several times: "Brother Saleh," then "Sardar Saleh." Why would a high-ranking member of the Pasdaran have traveled here? When he entered, he started to bound around the room. All that could be heard were his footsteps, whose curious rhythm evoked the gait of a crippled person. Then the footsteps drew nearer to me. He stopped moving when he got to me. Head lowered, facing the wall, I couldn't see anything but his khaki pants and his impeccably waxed military shoes. His body was nearly touching mine. He smelled clean, like a mausoleum, a mix of freshly washed sheets, rosewater, and jasmine. Then the sound of foot-steps started again as he walked toward Niloufar. Slowly. He lingered near her for a moment, before starting to pace again. The silence was disturbed only by a few distant, fearful whisperings. Niloufar had awoken. Her breathing had changed, like a freshly tuned violin. I sensed her stand up straight, then turn toward me, as if to assure herself that I was still there.

Sardar Saleh. Where had I heard that name? Who was this man? No doubt one of the former lords that the war had fabricated, one of those poor guys who come from nothing, modest teachers, taxi drivers, even bicy-cle repairmen, which accident, chance, or fortune had placed at the head of thousands of men. Then, once the war was over, they were at the height of power, they had been transformed into businessmen, mayors of big cities, prefects, governors. Curses in disguise for a society trying to reestablish peace.

For how long did he pace behind us? I couldn't tell you. Time seemed to stand still. Suddenly, a high voice, squeaky and authoritative, rung out. It wasn't addressing us but the others. He wanted to know the location and date of Niloufar's arrest. Then he asked a few questions regarding the state of her health. He asked if a doctor had examined her. Annoyed by the response, he swore, or, at least, cried out what could be called Quranic blasphemy, a particular exclamation used by the clergy or dignitaries of high rank. And he started pacing the room again. He approached me, got very close. His hand touched the bottom of my face. It was soft, plump, and warm. He then exerted a light pressure on my chin and lifted my head so I could see him. The man was large. He was wearing the uniform of officers of the Pasdaran army. His shirt was perfectly white, buttoned all the way to the top. I didn't dare look at his face, I could only see the lower half, with his gray beard, carefully clipped. He lifted my head a bit more. Then I made eye contact with him, fleetingly but sufficiently for his unusual face to imprint on my memory.

He was wearing a pair of black glasses, not sunglasses, but reading glasses with tinted lenses, for people with photophobia. His forehead was marred by a deep scar, a diagonal gash through the right eyebrow and visible even behind the dark lens of his glasses; it gave a threatening look to his face, which was barely softened by a light fold at the corner of his lips that seemed like the beginning of a smile but was in reality another scar.

For a moment, I had the impression that I had seen him before—even that he was someone I knew. I was almost certain. He stared at me for a moment, as if he were searching for something in my features. "Can you please tell me what your exact relationship is with Mademoiselle Niloufar Sedaghat?" he murmured in my ear in a clear, calm, almost respectful voice. I answered that Mademoiselle Sedaghat was my cousin. I didn't want to say any more about it: emphasizing our familial relation seemed sufficient to me, and inoffensive. But I was interrupted, and the beginnings of a smile floating on his face finally appeared. "That, I already know," he said. "I'd like for you to tell me about the nature of your relationship." I felt that I was losing my footing. "What relationship?" I asked him to specify, as if I didn't understand what he was insinuating. He began again, in a slightly agitated voice: "During the years '78 and '79, then the years that followed the revolution, you regularly went to the house of Monsieur and Madame Sedaghat, the parents of the mademoiselle. Can you tell me the reason?" I had to tell him something. I searched, but nothing came to mind. I could have told him that the Doctor was depressed, and I was taking care of his affairs, or else that Niloufar's mother had offered to give me piano lessons. Niloufar would have understood, she could have built on it. But I remained silent.

Faced with my silence, the man moved away from me and turned toward Niloufar. She was enveloped in a shapeless and dirty chador, beige, torn in places, made of a fabric with indecipherable patterns. The siren of the Caspian seemed far, so far away. She had raised her head and was looking at the man in charge with the eyes of a wounded fawn. They stared at each other for a moment. "Dear mademoiselle," Sardar Saleh suddenly said, without raising his voice, "describe for me your relationship with this man." As I had, she responded that I was a family member, that it was normal for members of the same family to visit each other, and that was all she had to say.

The limping giant acquiesced. The young woman's response seemed to conform to his expectations. Then he walked away. I heard him talking to another person. A moment later, the prison's head doctor entered. After a brief examination, he decided to take Niloufar for a more in-depth auscultation. Was that a good sign? Or the beginning of the end? The water that Muslims give the sheep to drink before slitting their throats? In any event, the room emptied. They had forgotten me, facing the wall, with a chair to my right. I remained seated and I waited.

I was alone for a good hour, perhaps longer. Then the room filled back up again. And the "tap, taap, tap, taap," of the cripple began again. They stood me up. I realized that I could turn my head, that I could look at the others. I couldn't help interpreting this as a bad sign. They had changed the layout of the chairs. Now I was facing the center of the room. Four men were in front of me. Sardar Saleh was standing near the door, arms crossed over his chest. He was looking at his underlings, pensive. He was waiting for something. I observed him discreetly. There was a strange, enigmatic *je ne sais quoi* about him. His features were blurred, as if the scars had scrambled them. Furthermore, he had to be younger than he seemed in his elegant uniform. Even the physical power he emanated seemed artificial. And his limp seemed to be less of a handicap than a nervous tic.

They brought Niloufar back in. She was walking slowly, stumbling slightly. White bandages encased her ankles, spotted here and there with the purple stains of the disinfectant. They had cleaned her face. They sat her next to me.

In the meantime, a table had been brought out, and a few folders placed on top of them, likely pieces of evidence, traces of our former existence, proof of our guilt. What had happened for us to deserve all this pomp, all this ceremony? The response to these questions was no doubt there, in front of us.

Suddenly, the room emptied, except for Sardar Saleh and an armed guard, who remained standing near the door. So this would be a three-player game. Let's get it over with, I said to myself, seeing the lame giant approach, then stand facing us, upright in his polished shoes. His eyes were on Niloufar as he walked toward me. There was something in his hand. It was an envelope containing a notebook. A small notebook, a hundred pages. I recognized it immediately, its blue plastic cover. He placed it on my knees.

"Are you the author of these theses?"

He was talking to me.

"Go on, look!" He ordered me.

I had no choice but to open it. From its uniform, tight lines, I recognized Niloufar's writing. It covered entire pages.

"So? Do you recognize it?"

Then I understood. Nilou had written everything, logged everything. The debates that I had led in their house, my discussions with Cyrus and the representative of the organization, which she must have listened to at the door, even our nightly exchanges, when, in her bedroom, she would ask me questions that I answered endlessly, for the sole pleasure of remaining near her, reveling in the sight of her shoulders, the scent of her hair, the gleam of her teeth. She had committed everything to memory, and then, patiently and meticulously, had transcribed everything in the blue notebook. But for what reason? For a book-length manifesto? A revolutionary manual? Did she think that by doing so she could destroy the old world and bring about a new one? Poor girl!

I might have been the only person on earth to have understood her eternal anguish. I knew that she had suffered in her own way, not from poverty or hunger, but from luxury, opulence. Deep down, she didn't want to change the world, but change worlds. She would have preferred a humble and honest father, rather than her powerful and arrogant one, a loving and simple mother, rather than her indifferent, elegant one. She would even have swapped her racing dog for a stray or a gutter cat. Her revolutionary fundamentalism stemmed from that, from her shame, her guilt, her regret. A sort of orthodoxy whose matrix was my words, the Marxist exegesis according to me, my fake engagement, my lies. So much deceit, draped in knowledgeable expressions and references, recycled again in theses and theories. I had helped her secretly fabricate the perfect anti-Chamkhaleh. I've already told you, what happened would never have happened without the contributions of us all. The worst crimes are committed with ideas; weapons only serve to fix them in blood.

I pretended to read a few lines. Then I raised my head. I had made my decision. I said I didn't know who had written these texts. That it wasn't me, in any case. Sardar Saleh's face took on a sardonic expression. As if he had been expecting that response.

"We should believe her then, if I'm understanding you correctly," he said, looking at me with an almost complicit eye. "She's the one who wrote them, is that right?"

Why ask me questions to which he seemed to already know the answer? As if he were expecting nothing other than my consent to send Niloufar to the gallows. She remained silent and impassive, like a sphinx, as if what was happening was of no concern to her, wasn't worthy of her attention.

Then the giant turned toward the table and grabbed another object, which he handed to me, saying: "And this? Do you recognize it? Is it yours?"

Of course I recognized it! How could I forget? It was during the effervescence of the revolt, at the moment of the shah's fall. In our town and its surroundings, all the police stations, the precincts, and the barracks had fallen to the hands of the revolutionary committee, which I had been a part of then, with the religious. To avoid conflict, the aforementioned committee wanted to stop the spread of weapons. Suddenly, a comrade grabbed my arm. "What about Chamkhaleh?" Shit! We had completely forgotten: Chamkhaleh had a gendarme barracks with twenty men. We rushed there immediately. Behind its locked doors and its high walls covered with barbed wire, the brick building seemed empty. Everything led us to believe that it had been abandoned; the only thing left behind, the royal flag flapping in the middle of the courtyard. We were almost at the entry gate when the bullets exploded through the air. Warning shots. From inside the barracks, someone ordered us not to come any closer. His accent betrayed him. It was the Azerbaijani commander of the barracks, the same one who had come in person to arrest poor Mohamad-Réza at the Doctor's house.

You see, I had to return to Chamkhaleh once more. As if everything that would happen and affect my fucking life would bring me back one way or another to that place. Once more, I found myself there, at the edge of the

213

Caspian Sea. The sky was low, the wind was blowing in gusts, crumpling the lion's mane on the flag hoisted on the flagpole, that lion that was turning red, unaware that the saber he was brandishing was already broken, and that the sun he was carrying on his back had just set forever.

We had tried to reason with the commander. I explained to him that it was over, that the king had fallen, that the army had aligned with the new regime . . . It was useless. He had given the order to his soldiers to fire at whoever entered the barracks. This went on for a little while. He finally agreed to surrender, on the condition that the new authorities granted safe passage, to him and to his men. But those new authorities were not yet in place. After several hours of negotiations, we ended up going to look for the imam of our town, the Friday preacher, a mullah influential enough for him to agree to surrender beneath his authority. I'll never forget that moment. The commander came out first. He emptied the magazine of his Uzi by firing into the air, then approached me with the firm gait of an officer and gave me a military salute. A real salute, with the stomping of the boots and puffed chest. The whole shebang. His uniform was impeccable, but his tired, red, and badly shaven face was drowned in tears. After standing immobile for a few moments, he removed his service weapon from his sheath, kissed it, and handed it to me, crying: "Long live the king!" It was his last valiant act as an officer of the royal army. I squeezed the cold metal of the pistol in my hand. On its butt was engraved, in gold letters, the phrase that he had just uttered: "Long live the king!" Coming back from Chamkhaleh, that night, we brought the revolutionary committee the weapons seized from the barracks. All the weapons except for one. The one that I was now holding in my hands: the Azerbaijani commander's Beretta, in an evidence envelope, with its "Long live the king!" engraved in gold letters on the butt.

And so years later, as a defenseless torture victim, I heard the desperate cries of the fallen officer reverberate in my head. The disgrace of a soldier who, unable to fight, had given up his weapon, to a scrawny novice and a turbaned mullah wearing babouches. A real tragedy!

So Niloufar hadn't destroyed it, that weapon, as she had claimed. For, yes, I'm the one who had given it to her, declaring with a theatrical seriousness that, when the moment came, the people would have to take power by force, because the capital would never abdicate without violence. Or something of the sort. I had hoped that, if we weren't able to liberate the people, or bring about the triumph of the working class, the Beretta would at least solidify my place in the heart of Nilou, my beloved Nilou.

Shit, we're fucked, I said to myself, that's how she got herself arrested. Then I heard Sardar Saleh's voice.

"This weapon doesn't belong to you either?"

He repeated his question several times, as if to assure himself that I had understood. In truth, I didn't know how to respond. With that weapon found on her, we no longer had a chance.

Sardar Saleh stared at me intensely. He glared at me from behind the lenses of his glasses, in which I saw the reflection of the room, Niloufar's face a luminous spot. The man seemed to be fixed on my lips, awaiting my response in the countdown of his breath. I felt a huge drop of sweat pearl on my temple and drip down my face. I turned toward Niloufar. Tears were clouding her eyes, without falling. She must have felt the weight of my gaze, for she turned toward me, too. She did it slowly. We observed each other for a moment. She guessed what I was going to say. Sardar Saleh was still awaiting my response, but with increasing impatience, tapping on his arm. I looked at the weapon again. Then I raised my eyes, I couldn't keep silent for much longer. And I shook my head in denial. There. It was over. Nothing was different from the moment before. My cowardice, my lie, my betrayal hadn't modified the course of time. The clock hands kept turning, like the earth.

§

Yes, my friend. That's the story I came here to tell you. You and no one else. You are, whether you like it or not, its guardian. It belongs to you now, you can do with it what you want. Tell it to others. To whoever wants to hear it. To whoever can pass it on. Why did I do it? To survive? I don't know. I've certainly thought about it every day since. I still don't know. But it is what it is. I did it.

"Do you mean to say that this weapon does not belong to you?" the officer said.

I shook my head once more, this time lowering my gaze.

"So you deny any relation with this woman," he said again, his voice suddenly vibrating with anger. "You mean to say that you have nothing to do with, with . . . "

He was seething, and I didn't know why.

"Do you know the danger you're putting her in?" he continued, in a higher voice.

He had addressed me informally. There was now no more room for manners, for decorum.

"Do you know the danger you're putting her in?" he repeated.

Of course I knew: I could be sending her to the gallows.

"And you, mademoiselle?" he said, turning toward Niloufar, who still seemed just as absent.

"Mademoiselle!" he shouted again.

That's when he grabbed her arm. It was an inconceivable gesture for a fervent Muslim, a high-level Pasdar on top of it. You never touch a woman! Then he grabbed her shoulders and shook her violently.

"Answer me, Ni-ni-ni-ni . . . " he cried out in a broken voice, as if he were out of breath. Like a pierced tire. My God! In a fraction of a second, the veil was lifted before my eyes. That stammering . . . the accent that only inhabitants of the North have, revealed . . . It was Mohamad-Réza! My childhood friend, the Majnun of Chamkhaleh, my eternal punching bag, the bashful and crazed lover of Niloufar, the worshiper who had written the name of his beloved on his chest with the edge of a broken glass, the phantom of the night, the stammering singer . . . It was him, there was no doubt, reemerging from oblivion. How had I not recognized him earlier?

"Nilou," he managed to say, finally, shaking his head with despair, and "my beloved," in a final exhale, audible only to my ears. The large sardar was stammering again; he who had stared down the barrel of a gun, gone up against bombs and shellfire, was flailing pitifully before a woman's name.

Niloufar had recognized him, too. She had buried her face in her hands and was crying. Like me, she had finally understood why we were there, why a general of the Pasdaran army was wasting time on two unimportant prisoners. Later, I learned that he had always been following me, since the night he had been caught in front of Villa Rose. When the gendarmes took him away, hopping ridiculously with his pants down, he had seen me, crouching in the shadows, squatting behind the property gate. From the beginning, he knew his Judas. He knew that it was me who had sold him out. And he had never forgotten for all of those years. He had stayed abreast of everything I had done. There was nothing he didn't know. My semi-clandestine activities at the end of the shah's reign, my involvement in my town's revolutionary committee, my role as troublemaker, as revolt leader, my Marxist-Leninist ideology courses, my collusion with the dissident organization in Tehran, my trips to Rasht, to the Doctor's house, my flight. Everything, he knew everything. After my arrest, he was the one who had made sure I stayed alive. He was awaiting his moment. It was Niloufar's arrest that had brought him out of the shadows. He was there to finally settle the score.

What followed is not very important. I'm sure you believe I paid for everything I did? Yes, I paid, with interest. I was beaten until I couldn't take it anymore, thrown in isolation, humiliated, deprived of sleep. But, unlike the others, I wasn't able to cry injustice. Do you think the ordeal inspired remorse, repentance? No. And do you know why? Because I continued to betray. And my final betrayal is you.

One day, the torture came to an end. Why? I don't know. Perhaps they deemed that I had been punished enough for my crime. They transferred me to another prison, where I was to rot for many long years, until my death perhaps. That's when you saw me arrive in your dark and humid cell. Remember, I was broken. I was nothing more than a clot of curdled blood and pus. I saw you emerge from your corner, creep up to me, fearful like a timid animal. You offered me the most precious thing that you had: your friendship. You took care of me, you bandaged my wounds, you fed me. Without your care, I probably wouldn't have survived. But you offered me something more. Something indispensable. You showed me unconditional love, without limits, without holding back. But I didn't reciprocate. I betrayed you with my distance, my coldness, my egotism. Why? Because deep down, I knew that I didn't deserve your love. Not any more than I deserved Niloufar's love, or the admiration of my peers.

Remember the day when they came to announce your release? You welcomed that event, which you had been awaiting for so long, with no joy. You left reluctantly, almost despite yourself, dragging your feet, as if they were taking you to the gallows. You left me a prisoner's most prized possessions: your clothes, your books, and your memories. I never forgot. Before leaving, you took me in your arms. You held me tight for a long time. Long enough that I could feel your interrupted breathing and your beating heart. You didn't cry the tears shining in the corner of your eyes. You said nothing, for you knew that your voice would betray you. It was better that way. But I stole even that last moment from you by looking away. I was afraid you would discover what I really am—a traitor.

§

Niloufar married Mohamad-Réza. No one seemed very surprised. It's true that there was no one left to remember the young girl who had turned the seashore upside down all by herself; the war and the repression had decimated the army and its followers. They got married after a pilgrimage to Mecca. The ceremony took place in our town. It was only at that moment that the inhabitants realized there was a person of influence among them, someone who belonged to the high spheres of power. That the stammering, timid child they had seen playing in the dust of the streets, who had left one day hanging from the door of a bus to join the battlefields of a war already nearly forgotten, had become an important sardar. The city was jammed from one end to the other, taken over by official cars, carrying high-ranking members of the Pasdaran army in uniform or high dignitaries of the regime, wearing dark suits with extra-long sleeves and shirts without collars or ties, buttoned to the top, unshaven cheeks, their foreheads all stamped by the brownish mark of the prayer. The wedding was organized in the strict tradition of official ceremonies of the new bigwigs: simple, no obvious pomp, no music. Apparently, no one saw Niloufar for the entire ceremony, not even the women. She had demanded that the act of marriage take place behind closed doors, with just a few close relatives. She said "yes" to the first call of the mullah and not to the third, as is customary. Then, the next day, the newlyweds left for an unknown destination. Probably to one of those secure residential neighborhoods in the capital city where the nomenklatura live.

As for me, I was eventually released. Do I owe it to Niloufar? Most likely. But, once out, I soon came up against invisible barriers. I had no more place in society: the doors of the university were closed to me, as were those of the administration. Even private companies refused to employ me. I went back to live with my parents. I spent my time smoking opium with Hossein—I held on thanks to that. Then, one day, I took the same road as my father had in the past, every morning. I walked along the river, then crossed the bridge, which was no longer made out of wood, but concrete. I passed in front of the windows of the jewelers, before reaching the row of tailors, approaching the door of my father's former shop, turning the key in the lock. The old panel of oxidized wood creaked on its rusted hinges. I headed toward the back of the shop and sat in front of the patinaed leather of my father's seat.

I became a tailor, then a silkworm merchant. I buried my parents. My father first, and my mother soon after. I stayed in their house. I spent my days sewing in the shop or in the farms, listening to the sound of the silkworms. I slept on a pile of clothes that had been commissioned and never collected, but that I kept just in case. I continued the family tradition. Little by little, the clients returned. My pants were as comfortable as those of my father.

Niloufar had two children. Then she disappeared, during a trip to Europe. She asked for political asylum in Sweden. She's lived in Malmö for five years, without her children, who she left in Iran. I heard she was working as a waitress in a bar in Södergatan, near the port. It's called the Seeburg. You see? It's the bar over there, at the end of that street, overlooking the sea. This is where my trip comes to an end. My trip, but not my story. For now that you've listened to me, now that you know the story of my life, I'd like to ask you to accompany me to the bar. Come on! It's cold, we'll warm up. There! Look, on the other side of the window, that woman with the faded hair and the overly made-up lips, with her low-cut blouse, standing behind the counter, under the neon lights. You see? That's her! That's Niloufar! My siren! Come on, let's go inside! She saw us. I'm sure she recognized me. I've finally found her again. Here she is. A few breaststrokes away from me. One last wave, and I'll be at her side. She'll take my hand and we'll dive together, into the ever darker blue of the depths.

NOTES

1   The traditional festival for the Iranian people who celebrate the Persian New Year on the day of the spring equinox; date varies from March 20 to March 22.

2   A Muslim who has made the pilgrimage, also known as the hajj, to Mecca.

3   A well-known prison, located near Karaj, twelve and a half miles from Tehran, where many political prisoners have been held, tortured, and executed since 1979.

4   The second Iranian communist party, founded in 1941. It maintained close relationships with the Communist Party of the Soviet Union. It was a major political party in Iran, banned under the shah after the American coup d'état in 1953, then active again beginning in 1979, until the purges under the Islamic Republic.

5   National hero of modern Persian history. He was the founder of a revolutionary movement based in the forests of Gilan, in Northern Iran, known as the "Jangal Movement." This uprising began in 1914 and continued until 1921, when the movement was dismantled, and Mirza Koochak Khan was assassinated following an agreement between Lenin and Reza Khan, the future Persian monarch.

6   The first republic, proclaimed by Mirza Koochak Khan in Rasht, the capital city of Gilan, in 1920 and overthrown in 1921.

7   The 28 Mordad (August 19) coup d'état took place at the culmination of secret operation "Ajax" led by the United Kingdom

and the United States, and executed by the CIA. Its aim was to restore the shah to his throne, in order to preserve Western interests in the exploitation of Iranian oil deposits by chasing out Mosaddegh, the Iranian Prime Minister, who had nationalized oil.

8 Remote and mountainous region of Gilan.

9 Literally "men of the woods."

10 Ayat al-Kursi is the 225th verse of the second surah of the Quran. It's reputed to calm all sentiments: fear, anger, and sexual desire.

11 September 8th, 1978.

12 February 13th, the day of the Iranian Revolution's victory. 22nd of the month of Bahman, according to the Iranian calendar.

13 Hossein Fatemi. An Iranian politician (1919–54). He was named Minister of Foreign Affairs in the government of Mohammad Mosaddegh, to whom he would be an ally. He was arrested after the fall of Mosaddegh, condemned to death, and executed.

14 A mountain overlooking the city of Langerood in Gilan.

15 The Iranian border point nearest to Basra, which was one of the main targets of Iraqi attacks and subject to heavy human losses.

16 One of the branches of Fadayiane Khalg, an extreme-left guerrilla movement.

ABOUT THE AUTHOR

JAVAD DJAVAHERY was forced to leave Iran at the age of twenty, escaping to France as a political refugee. He has never returned to Iran and now lives in Paris. In addition to writing screenplays and producing films, he has written two short-story collections in Persian and two novels in French. *My Part of Her* is his English-language debut.

ABOUT THE TRANSLATOR

EMMA RAMADAN is a literary translator based in Providence, RI, where she is the co-owner of Riffraff, a bookstore and bar. She is the recipient of an NEA Translation Fellowship, a PEN/Heim grant, and a Fulbright scholarship.

ABOUT THE INTRODUCER

DINA NAYERI is the author of *The Ungrateful Refugee*, a finalist for the 2019 Kirkus Prize. Her debut novel, *A Teaspoon of Earth and Sea* (2013), was translated into fourteen languages. Her second novel, *Refuge* (2017), was a *New York Times* editor's choice. She holds a BA from Princeton, an MBA from Harvard, and an MFA from the Iowa Writers' Workshop, where she was a Truman Capote Fellow and Teaching Writing Fellow. She lives in Paris, where she is a fellow at the Columbia Institute for Ideas and Imagination.